Willard Notch

Willard Notch

Ralph Zieff

Contents

Part I

THE NOTCH

Chapter 1

Jan and Rob

Jan Poschner emphatically pushed the jade green glass ashtray away from her and toward Rob Zanermann as he started to light up a joint, her way of saying "Not me, thank you" without having to say it.

"Oh, man, this weed is good," he said, after a deep inhalation of that delightfully pungent smoke that makes cottage cheese taste great, and "cutting the cheese" hilarious.

"Look," said Jan, "I don't intend to sit here with you and listen to your floating brain spit out giggles and goofy comments… Either you toss that weed, or I'm leaving. I thought we were really getting down to talking about us, our deeper shit. And now you're doing your typical escape thing as soon as it gets down to real feelings. Why are you doing that?"

Fifteen or twenty seconds elapsed before Rob responded, "I'm scared."

"Of what? Scared of what, Rob? The truth?"

"Oh yeah, the truth. And what truth is that, my dearest Janice?"

"Don't call me that. You know I hate it."

"What truth?" Rob repeated, without using the name Jan's parents would use when doing reprimands.

"That you don't really love me, Rob. I know you don't. I know you care about me a lot, but you care about Wendy, also, and it should be different with us." Jan's mentioning Rob's younger sister slowed down his response, making him pause and think for a moment. "You're wrong," he finally replied. "You don't understand how I feel about you. You don't."

"Then tell me! And not when you're in an 'I love everyone' happy haze!"

Jan jumped up from Rob's back porch patio table and strode off into his apartment, and then left through the front entrance.

As Rob heard her turning on her car and racing away, tires screeching a little, he felt helpless, stupid…and sad. His blue eyes, that Jan always called his "people-pleasing peepers" were now moist with tears and he had a terrible dull ache in his chest.

He thought to himself, "Dear God, I adore her… I love her so much… why can't I do a better job of telling her?" His mind flashed to a few things he loved about her that weren't exactly brother and sisterly, and he blushed. He spent many hours every day thinking about her, picturing her, and she was so clearly the most important thing in his life… and she didn't know it?

The weed haze he ordinarily loved was annoying him now, blocking him from truly embracing whatever it was that he was feeling.

"Fuck! Fuck, fuck it!" he exclaimed in a whispery shout, and then started to sob. He momentarily pictured himself as the hero guy in a romantic movie who takes off running after his girl's car, and actually catches up to it, pulls her out and kisses her passionately, telling her he does love her and will forever, and she cries as she allows his kiss to penetrate her soul. His arms moved as though he was wrapping them around her, leaning forward in the rusty green patio chair with the tubular white arms.

A cool breeze started blowing on this already cold, drizzly day, and Rob got up and went indoors, slamming the screen door.

* * *

It had been three years since the two had met, not all that long in terms of the big picture of one's life. The view from the helicopter, Rob's dad liked to call it. Ed Zanermann used to use that idea as a way to help Rob and Wendy not get too upset when something negative happened, such as when Marsha, their mom and his wife, suddenly, with no warning, left home, left Willard Notch, and even left New Hampshire, with Andy Hauser, her personal trainer (Ed, Rob, and Wendy all got to hate that slightly ironic title, and snickered when hearing it from anyone). Andy, who was only eight years older than Wendy (and "unbearably cute," Wendy's friends would say), had moved to Willard Notch the year before from Rochester, New York, and seemed to have made a beeline for Ed Zanermann's beautiful wife. This all happened ten years ago.

"I know this must feel like a humongous tragedy in your lives right now—and in mine, too—but someday, when you're looking at the big picture of your life from that helicopter in the sky, it won't seem as big, and your lives will have so many other things happening, some good, mostly, and some bad, too. You'll see it from a different perspective, and it won't feel as awful as it does now."

The first few times Ed told his kids that, he couldn't help breaking into tears, but over the years all three of them managed to talk about it dry-eyed. Wendy and Rob were helped by lots of letters and occasional visits from their mom and Andy (with whom they still never felt comfortable), but their dad? Well, that was a different story. Everyone in Willard Notch all agreed that Ed Zanermann had never recovered from that big blow he received ten years earlier, and they were right.

4

It was now three years for Rob and Jan, and while it really only took him two months to know that she was the woman he wanted to marry and be with forever, it took her quite a bit longer.

She, as women tend to do, needed time to sort out some issues about Rob, in terms of what kind of father he would be (his role model, his dad, was a kind man, a sweet man, and one who certainly took his kids' feelings more seriously than his deserting wife did), his career aspirations and life goals (she didn't know those because he himself didn't know them), his pot smoking, (which he appeared to have pretty well under control), and the kind of lover he was (which was very attentive and giving, and someone with whom she always felt safe). Over time she grew convinced she loved this good man, and knew she wanted to be his wife someday. So with Rob, what mattered was how much he wanted her, more than any other girl he had ever known, and with Jan it was what a good life partner he would make. They were both Jewish, although not very religious, and both families felt good about their being in an exclusive relationship.

Jan's parents still seemed to be a happily married couple after twenty-two years of marriage, and both lavished lots of love and attention on their only child. Carl and Beverly Poschner were one of the most popular couples in Willard Notch, being very outgoing and active in the community, and while Beverly had served for thirteen years on the District 14 School Board, quitting only after Janice had gone off to UNH in Dover, Carl still served as the Menard County Commissioner of Public Safety, a role he truly relished. When there had been talk of Ed Zanermann going after Andy Hauser with a rifle, it was Carl who got to Ed and talked him out of it before the County Sheriff, Troy Dobson, got to him. Ed, who owned the town's only men's clothing store, eventually expressed to Carl his feelings of gratitude, but it took him a while. Since the big scandal years ago with Marsha and Andy, Ed had been rather subdued in any matters dealing with women and dating—unenthusiastic, people would say—but most also knew that he had a huge "soft spot" (or "hard on," depending who was talking) for Beverly Poschner, a fact that had grown extremely awkward for him with the development of Rob's and Jan's romance. That Beverly tended to think of Ed only as a "very nice man" kept that awkwardness to a minimum, and neither Rob nor Jan knew anything of Ed's secret yearning.

* * *

Jan was hoping Rob would call or text her or even come to the house, but she also knew how unlike him that would be.

She knew she would have to be the one to reach out, apologize for leaving so abruptly, and ask him how he was doing since their "talk". Only this time, she wasn't sure she was going to do that. For once, she thought, he should "man up" and reach out to her, and if he wasn't willing to do that, let there be silence... for as long as he needed to avoid her. Jan was keenly aware of how easy she had been making things for him over the course of their relationship. Too easy... so easy that he's never had to come face to face with his feelings for her, and what losing her would mean to him. Perhaps it was time to change all that. Determined to resist reaching out to Rob, she called her best friend, Ashley Seznicky, and simply said, "I'm on my way over."

Ashley Seznicky was considered by everyone to be the most beautiful young woman in Willard Notch. Her Polish father and Colombian mother had produced three gorgeous children, two drop dead gorgeous boys, and then Ashley. She was not in a relationship these days, but was developing a crush on Larry Boynton, Willard Notch's premier athlete (quarterbacked three years at UNH and one of the best golfers in school history). Larry was a ruggedly handsome African American young man, and while powerfully built, was unusually gentle and respectful toward the many females pursuing him, many of whom wished he was less gentle with them. Being black in New Hampshire was not much different than in any other place, with a very mixed bag of experiences. While he was revered and rewarded whenever athletics was involved, long unpleasant stares and occasional racist remarks were common when one of Willard Notch's supposedly virginal white girls (and clearly non- virginal women) was flirting with him. That complication had kept him rather low key about females when in town (although that beautiful Seznicky girl had begun to get his attention), and his only romance had been with a black girl in nearby Benson, a relationship that lasted a year until she and her family moved to Connecticut a year ago. As for sexual relationships, there had been a multitude of those on campus in Dover. He, like most other handsome college sports stars had a veritable playground spread out (pardon the pun) before him.

"So what's goin' on?" Ashley asked Jan, as they sat on a two-seater swing sofa on her front porch.

"Guess!" Jan retorted.

"Rob," Ashley surmised. Jan responded only with a feeble smile.

* * *

Rob was sitting on the edge of his bed with his head in his hands, and still muttering to himself about being such a disgusting wimp with Jan. Thinking of losing her, of her rejecting him in disgust, was making him nauseous, literally… and he didn't dare leave the house feeling that way. He knew he needed to call his dad at the store and tell him he wouldn't be doing his usual late Wednesday shift at Zanermann's Men's Shop. Wednesday was the only night they stayed open until 9:00 in an attempt to push back a little at the Notch Mall's big box stores that stayed open until 9:00 six nights a week. He felt bad about doing it because he knew his dad would then call Wendy, ask her to fill in for Rob, and she would say she couldn't, that she had plans with her friends (probably a weed party) she couldn't break.

Rob knew his dad would not argue with her, and not complain to her about having to work a twelve hour day. He never did either of those with Wendy. He always seemed to be afraid to fight with her, afraid she would shut him out, a fear he didn't seem to have whenever he argued with Rob, which they did sometimes, but not that often. H e knew his dad wouldn't complain about long hours in the store, because ever since his wife ran off with that piece of "Handy Dandy Randy Andy Candy" as he liked to call him, he sometimes seemed happier in the store than at home. With business down quite a bit, it could be deadly boring at the store, and Rob wondered how his dad spent his time in the often empty store. Rob knew his dad felt very attached to the store because his grandfather had started the business, and passed it on to Ed at a time when business was very good, and Ed never said a bad word about his father. Rob was aware that he himself was very connected to his dad, also, but he was never really aware of just how deeply.

Rob got an apple out of the refrigerator, and went back out to the porch, where he could still feel Jan's aura.

Chapter 2

Ed Zanermann and The Night Visitor

Ed was in his back room office located behind the two customer dressing rooms. The musty room contained a bell hook-
up that would signal him if anyone came into the store. The
antique brass desk lamp with the emerald colored shade was
on, and shining down on three 4x6 unframed photographs he
was staring at, seated in the old walnut swivel desk chair his
dad had used for 44 years before his accidental death, and that
Ed himself had used ever since. His head was fairly close to the
three photos, and his body appeared to be trembling or spas-
ming as he uttered small muted sounds that indicated he was
in the throes of some kind of intense experience. The fact that
his right hand was well inside his Maurice Fabrizio grey flannel
slacks and pumping rapidly left no doubt what type of intense
experience it was. Ed finished his coital simulation with a gasp
and an "Oh god" attached to it, as his head slumped on top of
the three well-worn photos. One was of Marsha, one of "Handy
Dandy Randy Andy," and one was of Beverly Poschner. The sig-
nificance of those three photographs was quite clear, and left
little room for conjecture about what his thought process might
have been while engaging with them, but the frequency of those
engagements was a little startling, and did invite some conjecture as to Ed's inner workings.

"Gosh, Dad, I'm really sorry," Wendy Zanermann told Ed. "The girls are putting on this party because it's Mary Ann's birthday on Sunday, and I can't not be there.

"Okay honey, have a good time. I'll be fine."

"Thanks, Daddy. I really wish I could. Don't wait up for me. I'm sure I 'll be late."

"Okay honey. I love you."

"I love you, too."

Ed closed his cell phone and put it into his elegant and still slightly warm Italian crafted pocket, and went out into the front of the store, having heard the bell ring.

"Hello. Welcome to Zanermann's," Ed said to the strikingly handsome stranger who had just entered his store.

"Hello," the man replied tersely, leaving Ed—"Supersalesman Ed," as Marsha used to call him—to figure out if the man was cold or shy. Ed used his handkerchief to wipe a little remaining sweat from his simulation off his forehead.

"Are you looking for anything in particular, or would you like to just look around, and if you have any questions, I'm here?"

The man didn't answer for about ten seconds, and then muttered, "Yeah".

"Great," replied the supersalesman, assuming the stranger acquiesced to the second part of his question. "Just let me know if I can help."

"No," the man retorted, "I'm looking for something in particular."

"Oh, I'm sorry. I misunderstood you"

"Yeah, I figured that out."

Well, it's cold, not shy, Ed thought to himself.

"So what is it you're looking for?"

"It's not what, it's who."

"Who?"

"Yeah, who."

"Well who are you looking for?"

"The person in Willard Notch New Hampshire who has the internet user name 'Randycandy.' "

Ed immediately became aware of his heart starting to pound, and started sweating like he was into another simulation.

"Do you know him?" the stranger continued. "The guy was online seeking some information about my services, but disappeared before we could get some negotiations going... Do you know Randycandy?"

Ed was sure he saw a very slight smirk on the man's face as he asked that last question.

"What kind of business are you in?" he asked, and he was sure this guy could hear how shaky his voice was.

"That's between me and Randycandy. So do you know him or not?"

"Why did you come here to ask me that?" The man just stared back at Ed, eyes like lasers, and said nothing.

"Did someone tell you I'm Randycandy?" Again, the man said nothing, but a slight smile was developing on the left side of his mouth and his eyes widened a little.

"Look," said Ed, who was now supremely uncomfortable, to the point of being both very sweaty and having a bone dry mouth, "I've got things I have to do, so if this is as far as we can go, I think you should ask at another store."

"Well I do need to buy a black leather belt, size 40. How about that?"

Ed sighed, and said, "Yeah, sure, we do have one that size and color. I'll get it for you."

Ed went behind a large wooden display case that held belts, wallets, three boxes of white linen handkerchiefs a few pens, one cigarette lighter, and three bottles of a mid-priced British men's spray cologne, opened a draw and pulled out a long, thin box that had four belts in it, all size 40, and one of them black with a silver metal buckle. "You can pay for it over here, and I'll wrap it up for you," said Ed as he strode over to a glass case near the entrance to his back office that had on it a cash register, a device for credit cards, about a half dozen paper bags with the Zanermann logo (a large Z encircled with the words "Men's Clothing and Accessories of the Finest Kind",) and a pad of blank receipts, something he used occasionally when his register didn't print out a legible one.

Ed was very aware that he was too rattled at the moment to function as the super salesman that Marsha and his father always said he was. He hoped the man wouldn't notice that he was rushing the sales process… that he had not shown the belt to his customer, extolling the virtues of the item… AND, he had not even told him the price. He hoped this scary guy would just buy and go, but that was not to be. As Ed hastily reached for a paper bag for the still unwrapped belt, the Ice man reached out with snake-like speed and tightly gripped Ed's wrist, leaning forward and hissing through gritted teeth, "Listen, Fucko, I think *you* are Randycandy! What do you think?" Ed could only muster up a weak, groaning admission that he was.

* * *

Several weeks before the ice man cometh, Ed had been surfing his usual sites, Modern Men's Fashions and Horny Housewives, when he somehow stumbled over a website about contract killers, their increasing presence in America, and the high frequency of contracts on spouses, both former and present. A few days later he became aware of how much his thoughts were drifting toward a revenge fantasy in which he arranged the deaths of one, the other, or both of that beloved couple, Marsha and Handy Randy, picturing each on a floor with blood oozing from their respective heads. He focused more often on the Candy man, because, after all, Marsha was Rob and Wendy's mother, and he did love his kids. While in that rather violent and morbid part of Cyberland, Ed had pursued a few links until he found himself on a site that actually gave the user a chance to ask questions of real paid assassins. He had simply typed in "Services in New Hampshire? #Randycandy," waited for a few minutes, got no response laughed at his own gullibility, and left the site, not at all aware of the door he was opening.

* * *

The handsome stranger stepped out of Zanermann's Men's Shop into the nippy night air so common in Willard Notch, and strode off toward his black Jaguar, noticed by no one because the streets were empty except for two noisy stray dogs howling at the bright half moon glowing above Town Hall. As his car sped off into the night, the "CLOSED" sign was being placed in the window of Willard Notch's only men's clothing store.

* * *

Ed's three year old silver Honda Accord beat a hasty path toward his home in Wicker Falls, a small, sleepy suburb just over the Willard Notch town line. He was upset almost to the point of vomiting, and he was sweating profusely even though the night air was chilly. He felt the vibration of the small black flip phone in his pocket, telling him of an incoming call. and while he was tempted to let it ring, he, as always, answered it. His "What if one of the kids needs me?" mantra dictated that he answer.

"Hello?"

"Hi, Dad"

"Hey, Rob m'boy," he answered, trying to sound normal, even though he was feeling anything but.

"Are you okay?"

Ed froze for a minute, reacting as though he just discovered Rob had been peeping through his tiny ground level office casement window when he was with the Iceman. Or before.

"Yeah, sure. Why?"

"No, I was just wondering because I know you've just been working one of those god-awful twelve hour days."

"Ah, well, thanks for thinking of me, but I'm fine. Almost home."

"Okay, Dad. G'night."

"You too, Rob m'boy. You, too."

Ed closed his phone slowly, thinking to himself what a great kid Rob was, how close they have always stayed, maybe almost too close? And how much alike they were, something of which Ed Zanermann was only partially aware.

Chapter 3

Ashley and Jan, Wendy and Larry

Mary Ann Wolcott's birthday party was just ending at 11:00, and Wendy Zanermann said her good nights to everyone there and stepped into the now cold night air. Why her parents had chosen to raise their family in New Hampshire rather than Florida, or California, or even Atlanta, she'd never know. As she started walking toward her house in Wicker Falls, which was actually only a five minute walk, she didn't notice the black Jaguar parked in the pitch dark tree shadows on Falls road.

What she did notice was two young females, too far away for facial recognition, but one definitely with Ashley Seznicky's voice, laughingly saying to the other girl, "I can't believe you just said that… Not you… You're such an old lady!" The response to that was too softly spoken for Wendy to be able to identify the voice. Part of her wanted to run up to the two, and jump into the fun, but for some reason she also considered staying back and listening to more. Maybe it was that the second girl spoke so softly, as though there was something clandestine about their interaction. There it was, "clandestine," that dumb word that had knocked her out of Miss Horton's eighth grade spelling bee some years ago because she left out the "e" at the end. T hat stupid letter really served no earthly purpose, as her 87-year-old grandmother, Bubbie Zanermann, used to say about punk rock and pit bulls. Again, Ashley's voice was very audible when she said, "C'mon, you know he's gorgeous, and what have you got to be afraid of?"

"It's not what, it's who!" the other girl responded, and Wendy's jaw dropped in instant recognition that it was Jan Poschner's voice. She really liked her brother's girlfriend, and often wondered why he hadn't already married her, or at least become engaged to her. But this shadowy little scenario gave her some negative vibes, and in fact, aroused enough suspicion for her to stay in her eavesdropping mode.

"Cmon, Jan! You aren't afraid of Rob, and you know it!"

"I'm not afraid of him. He's a sweet guy, but I don't want to hurt him, and I'm not at all sure I want to lose him."

"He doesn't need to know."

Ashley's words triggered a pang of anxiety in Wendy, and she began inching closer to the shadowy scene, wanting to be sure to hear Jan's response. Wendy loved her brother dearly, and while he could be a jerk sometimes, she knew he didn't deserve any mistreatment from Jan. And besides, one wounded guy in the family was enough. She could see on a daily basis the aftermath of an unfaithful woman just by glancing at her dad. If he knew you were looking at him he would appear okay, but if he thought no one was, his thinly veiled pain and anger were evident. Wendy was no naive kid, and there wasn't much question given things Jan had already said that she was up to no good.

"Look, Ash, he is really hot, and it could be fun, but…"

"But nothing," interrupted Ashley," and he also does have a great butt, you must admit."

"Have you been with him before?" Jan asked.

"No, but I have a cousin who went to UNH, and she was, along with a few hundred others, and she said it was an unforgettable experience, between his beautiful face, muscles everywhere, great butt, and a ridiculous cock. She said girls would be after him all the time, and that he once did all ten cheerleaders on the same night at a party. He likes to be with multiples, so you and I would really appeal to him."

"He must have an ego bigger than his cock ," Jan offered.

"Yeah, I'm sure he's very egotestical," Ashley added, and both girls broke into giggles over Ashley's ironic slip of the tongue, and when Ashley referred to it as that, they giggled even more over that double entendre.

Wendy was now very upset, and considered coming out of the shadows and confronting these two queens of raunch, but she wanted to hear more, and learn what guy they were talking about.

"So what are we doing?" Ashley sounded irritable, her impatience getting the better of her.

"God, Ash, I don't know. Don't leave it up to me... please!"

"Okay! Alright! I'm calling him now!" Ashley grabbed her phone out of her jacket pocket and prepared to make her call.

"No, wait, not yet."

"Yes, Jan, right now!" Within a minute, Ashley was beginning her daring call.

"Larry? Hi, this is Ashley Seznicky. Yeah...yeah... How are you? Do you think I'm crazy calling you like this at this time of night? Oh...good...yeah... You know we don't really know each other, but Jan Poschner and I were out drinking earlier, and now we're sort of high with nothin' to do, and then I thought of you... Larry! No, well, I mean yes...we were, and we both think you're very hot, and... Really? Are you sure? Great... Yeah, I know where that is... We'll be there in a half hour... Yeah, great...bring some with you."

"Bring what?" Jan whispered.

"Weed. What did you think it was?"

"Condoms," Jan giggled.

Wendy was not giggling. Nor was she smiling. And not feeling even slightly amused.

"Hey listen, Jan. There's something we should talk about."

"What?"

"You and me."

"What?"

"You and me. You know, like how close do you and I want to get?"

Ashley could tell from Jan's facial expression that 1) That thought never crossed her mind, and 2) She had never been in a threesome, at least not with another girl.

"All right, listen," Ashley went on, putting a comforting hand on Jan's shoulder. "If Larry wants to head in that direction, I'll just tell him not tonight, dude, you're all we want right now, and he'll be fine. He's cool."

The look of relief on Jan's face told her she had guessed right. "C'mon, let's go get my car," she said, and the two girls started walking toward her light blue Toyota Matrix. Wendy stayed where she was as the two drove off, almost frozen in place, emotionally reeling from the outrageous scene she had just witnessed. "Just wait until Rob hears about this," she muttered to herself, now continuing toward home, but by the time she got to the house, she was already seriously reconsidering whether or not to tell him.

One wounded man in her life was definitely enough.

Chapter 4

The Zanermanns

When Wendy got inside the house, the first thing she saw was her dad sitting on one of their retro yellow Naugahyde and chrome kitchen chairs, his head in his hands, his elbows on their Formica kitchen table. Marsha Zanermann had a thing for retro kitchens (and sexy personal trainers, apparently), and had come home one night from a good old fashioned New Hampshire country auction with the table and the four "daisy chairs" as Ed always snickeringly called them. Most of their home had been decorated by Marsha, and much of that was subject to "Edwardian" snickers, that being as close as he ever got to an argument with her about anything.

It wasn't that he was "pussy-whipped," as some whispered, but rather, Wendy often thought, "pussy-dependent." Her mom never had to browbeat her dad into anything, just express a need or a wish, and her husband would always aim to please (apparently except when it ultimately came to her appetite for Randy Andy).

"Hi, Dad, what's going on?"

Wendy's voice made Ed spring up, plaster one of those anemic half-smiles on his face, and blurt out, "Oh, hi, Honey. How was the party?"

"It was okay. Nothing very exciting, but I enjoyed it."

"You always enjoy being with your friends, don't you," he responded, "certainly more than you enjoy Zanermann's!"

"Oh, Daddy, I hope you're not upset about my not working tonight. I really appreciated your telling me I could go to the party."

Wendy som etimes called him "Daddy" when in a very good mood or in a very pro-Dad conversation; she knew it made him feel good that his big girl still had in her some of the little girl who idolized him. She always figured it helped him deal with his sad reality that her mom was rarely verbally validating or romantic with him. God, every man she's ever known, her father and brother being great examples, needs to feel female admiration. Her mind darted to Larry Boynton and the likelihood that he was feeling extremely admired, right about now.

The sound of a car pulling into their driveway got both to turn toward the front door, and a moment later Rob came in like a Sherman tank, saying, "Hey you two, I'm going up to the guest room. I don't feel like talking, but I'll come back down later."

It all happened so quickly that neither Ed nor Wendy had a chance to say anything, and they agreed that while it was clear that something was going on with Rob, it was impossible to tell what it could be.

"Guest room?" Ed queried.

"C'mon Dad, you know he's talking about that room you still call his. You never seem to let go of him and accept the idea that he's a grown man, living his own separate life in his own separate place. He's not moving back in. Ever."

"Listen, darling daughter, he hasn't exactly developed a productive life out there. But I suppose he'll do better when he and Jan get married, if they do. She's really good for him, helps him think things through, gives him more confidence."

Wendy felt a cold chill run through her at the mention of Jan 's name. Yeah, oh sure, she's great for his self-esteem. If Rob knew what she was up to right now, he would probably jump off the I-95 bridge in Portsmouth.

"Hey, there's still a few of those little cupcakes in the fridge. Want some with some tea?"

"No, thanks, Dad. I'm good. But I do want to go upstairs and talk to Rob about a few things before I go to bed."

Wendy headed upstairs, nervous about what she should or shouldn't say to Rob about Jan. It felt like she had a dirty little secret to share, and she worried about how the big brother she loved so much would react to the news. Her mind flashed to some especially painful moments with her dad for months after her mom ungraciously announced to him that she was leaving him to be with Andy. She couldn't bear the thought of Rob being that devastated, that wounded, and that angry. And yet she felt that he needed the truth. In fact, she owed it to him.

Rob had long been Wendy's "big brother protector," as everyone in the family had sometimes called him. It was Rob who had fought and beaten Moose Swayheart in the high school courtyard after the big center on the freshman basketball team had taken an impulsive swing at her when she told him she was going on a date with Jason Goldberg, the class "genius". Moose was actually an okay kid, but no one was going to threaten Rob Zanermann's little sister and get away with it.

And then there was the time back when Wendy was in the second grade that Rob went with her to the principal's office to explain that it was accidental when she stepped on and ruined Billy McGinnis's "show and tell" Boston Celtics Kelly green pennant he had proudly brought to school the day after he had been at the Garden to see the "C's" crush the Detroit Pistons.

Billy had leaned it against Wendy's seat after he displayed his Leprechaun-blessed treasure and was expounding on how great Boston's NBA entry was. Wendy got up to go next when Billy was finishing to scattered applause, and unceremoniously put a huge crease in the delicate felt, causing Billy to gush tears and scream "You bitch!" at Wendy, probably a subtle message he had heard his dad yell at his mom many times over (Willard Notch's rumor mill had long ago pegged Ted McGinnis as the town's most abusive husband). Wendy, in turn, threw a wicked punch that landed squarely on Billy's chest that made a resounding thud, and induced a frantic "Ow! I'm gonna' kill you, you bitch!" (more home schooling, most likely). Miss Doherty, the Second Grade teacher, banished Wendy to the Main Office for hitting, assuming Assistant principal Paul Willard (the Notch was obviously not above nepotism) would appropriately discipline the little Jewish ruffian (The Doherty family attended St. Mary's Church, as did the McGinnises). However, Rob, who had heard of the altercation in his Fifth Grade classroom during snack break, ran down to the Office and gave Mr. Willard a very persuasive explanation of Wendy's innocence of bad intentions As a result, Mr. Willard said he would have to put the incident in Wendy's "folder" (the private official document for millions of elementary school kids that kept a running account of achievements… and sins), but would not take any further action against her.

Wendy's mind briefly flashed to the moment her fist had gloriously landed on Billy's chest, and Mr. Willard's subsequent pardon, and with a warm smile on her face, knocked on the guest room door. "What!" Rob responded.

"It's me, Rob. Lt's talk."

"Not now, Wen. Maybe later."

"How about now, Rob. There's something we need to talk about."

"It can't wait?"

"No."

"So, what is it?"

Wendy entered the room and proceeded to share with Rob all that she overheard from Jan and Ashley. "Godammit!" Rob bellowed. "I knew I never liked Jan spending time with that whore

Ashley." Wendy blinked in amazement that Rob's first thought wasn't about Jan, or Larry… or even himself, but about Ashley. "Godammit!" he repeated, but this time with less anger and more anguish. "I've tried to be a better communicator for her, but holy shit, this is what she does to me?" Wendy felt a little relieved that Rob was now focusing on his girlfriend's infidelity, the most important issue in this mess.

As Wendy watched and listened, her big brother ran through a potpourri of emotions, with nasty anger and whimpering anguish the predominant ones. At one point, Rob started laughing almost hysterically, which freaked Wendy out a little, but he eventually put words to it that revealed it to be about the irony of him grappling all day with whether or not to ask her to marry him.

"No fucking way!" he bellowed at one point. But then there was that other moment, a very creepy one, where he was again laughing, but this time with a sort of evil cackling sound. Wendy noticed no response from her father, who actually was now in the basement at his old beat up desk, and unable to hear the noise upstairs, or maybe just preoccupied?

"I've gotta get out of here, Wen. I need fresh air. Tell Dad I said goodnight and that I'm okay."

"Are you?" Wendy asked.

"Absolutely," Rob responded. "G'night, Wen. Thanks for telling me what happened." He went out the front door into the cold dark Wicker Falls Fall night air.

* * *

Rob's mind was inundated with images of Jan singing to him, making love to him, laughing, crying together, banging Larry, laughing hysterically with Ashley, giving him a haircut, banging Larry, helping him with the bandages after his foot surgery, banging Larry… and his rapid, intense breathing sent a billowing mist into the night air. As he picked up his pace and began muttering to himself. He was totally unaware of the sleek black Jaguar that had pulled out of the shadows, and was very slowly following behind, with no lights on. He went on for several more blocks, and then except for the sound of a car door opening and closing, all was quiet in Wicker Falls, the cozy little suburb of Willard Notch.

Chapter 5

The Poschners

Jan used her key to go in the front door of the Poschner's modest Willard Notch home, assuming her parents were likely already asleep. She quickly discovered she was right. All the lights were out in the house, a little surprising because they usually left the front hall light on as a night light.

Since some of her dates with Rob went pretty late and her parents were not late night people, except if they were partying with friends, and since tonight she was later than usual, she missed having the light illuminating the door lock and the threshold of the little vestibule, but she managed. She walked quietly into the kitchen, and pulled out a blue-capped orange juice bottle, poured a half glass after shaking it to spread that lovely pulp, and quickly downed that half glass of sunshine, as they described it in TV ads.

She sat at the kitchen table for a while, running the night's events through her mind. Her doing that was a continuation of her hour long "processing," as they liked to call it, with Ashley. Jan had learned that term she now shared with Ashley (she and Rob NEVER processed; he wasn't open enough for that... he called the term psycho-babble) from the counselor she had seen during the wretched aftermath of her contracting mono in her junior year of high school.

Ashley and Jan had agreed the encounter with Larry, as hot as it was, had also gotten pretty uncomfortable, and it took them a while to compare notes and talk things out.

They seemed to agree that things turned from hot to uncomfortable as it became evident to both girls that Larry, who was everything they thought him to be, kind, thoughtful, gentle, and extremely gorgeous physically, had a real yen for Ashley, and not at all as much for Jan. He did his best to hide that reality, and Ashley tried to deflect some of his passion toward Jan, but after a while it became clear to all three of them that Larry was wishing he could be alone with Ashley. It was to his credit, Jan tried to assure the apologetic Ashley, that the fact he could have his feelings focus on one woman instead of on playground kink was a definite plus, and she encouraged Ashley to call him in the morning and acknowledge the connection.

"You're sure you're not upset?" Ashley asked.

"Absolutely, positively!" assured Jan. "He is quite the specimen, Ash, and oh my god, that first stroke took my breath away, but I immediately had misgivings about what I was doing because of Rob. I do really love him, a lot. And I was a little relieved when Larry refocused on you. I think he really digs you, and you looked like you were quite into it all."

In the darkness of Ashley's car, Jan couldn't see the intense blush that spread through her best friend's face Jan smiled a little, thinking how cool it would be if Ash and Larry became a couple, maybe even got married and had kids, and she would know all along that she had been there at the moment it all began! As she got up from the table and headed for the upstairs she giggled over her wacko thought that they would have a little girl they named Larshley Janice Boynton, and that she agreed to be little Larshley's godmother. She quietly made her way to her room, feeling very sleepy. As she approached the door of her parents' bedroom, she wondered if this was one of those nights when Carl and Beverly Poschner "retired" (what a stupid word, she thought) to their bedroom earlier than usual, with Carl flashing his horny wet-eyed look at his wife, and she giving him an almost secret little smile in response. Their door was ajar, she noticed, as she passed their room, so Jan expected to find Lebowski curled up on her bed, waiting for her. When she got to her room, there was no Maine Coon cat named Lebowski (named after the Coen Brothers cult movie classic) on the bed. Or anywhere. Too tired to do anything about it, Jan Poschner fell onto her bed face first and quickly fell asleep.

* * *

The sunlight splashing into Jan's bedroom woke her up. Ordinarily it would be Lebowski's rough little tongue as he licked the salt off her cheek, but posing as a genius feline alarm clock. "Lebo's tongue," as Jan liked to call it, really was like clockwork, and her first thought of the new day was, "Where is Lebo?" While still on the bed, she made that pursed lips sucking sound that people always do with cats (and some nasty guys with females). "Lebo? Lebo? Lebowski, where are you, big boy?"

When Lebowski didn't come, Jan got irritated and got out of bed to go and find him. As she went down the hallway, she again came to her parents' room, knocked, went in, and immediately started shrieking at the sight of Beverly and Carl Poschner, her mom and her dad, lying side by side on their blood-soaked bed, wide-eyed but sightless, together but lifeless. Stone cold dead, both of them. Each body had many cuts and slashes, with darkened congealed blood formed around most of them.

Jan continued to shriek for several minutes (her throat would probably burn and ache for days after), and then started screaming, "Help me, someone please help me! Oh Mom…oh my god… Daddy… Please… PLEASE!" She fell to the floor, not losing consciousness, but feeling the effects of have lost bladder control and feeling her stomach churning from the dank, sour smell of blood that had become overwhelmingly sickening.

"Hello? Who's here? Do you need help? It's Maggie, Beverly. Are you okay?"

It was the voice of Maggie Hartley, the Poschner's next door neighbor of sixteen years, and she was yelling from the downstairs vestibule.

"Maggie, Maggie. Help me, please. HELP ME!"

Maggie responded, "Oh, Jan. I'm coming, I'm coming."

She was to tell Sheriff Dobson later that morning that she had found Jan on the floor screaming and sobbing intermittently, disheveled and shaking. Maggie had the wisdom to grab a blanket from the top of the cedar chest in the Poschner master bedroom, and wrap it around Jan and held her as she dialed 911. They sat on the floor in silence for a few minutes as they waited for Troy Dobson and one of his deputies to arrive, along with Al Fenton, the county forensics guy.

Maggie, Troy, and Jan were now seated at the kitchen table, all three sipping tea that Maggie had prepared in large "Willard Notch Department of Athletics" purple ceramic mugs. The team colors of the Willard Notch Jaguars were purple and white, and the High School, which served the Notch, Wicker Falls, and Sawyer, had been having very successful years of late, just missing a Granite State Championship in football a few years back in Larry Boynton's Senior year at quarterback.

"Troy, honey, I think you need to give Jan, here, a little time to be able to discuss what she found… this poor girl is still in shock. As Maggie uttered those words of advice to Menard County's very popular Sheriff, Jan burst into tears that lasted for at least a full minute, and then said in a very shaky voice," You saw what I found, Sheriff Dobson," and then burst into tears again.

She leaned forward until her head rested on her hands which were lying crisscrossed on the kitchen table. After several minutes of total silence, Eunice Dobson's younger son, a tall and ruggedly handsome 37 year old man elected Sheriff three times already, cleared his throat, rose from his seat, and said, "Look, Jan. You do need to tell me everything you remember about this morning, and I do mean everything, and I'll be back like around seven this evening so you can do that. Maggie, I trust you'll take good care of her until then."

"I will, Sheriff, I will," said Maggie, a little annoyed at Troy's lack of empathy.

Maggie Hartley, who was the same age as Beverly Poschner, with their Leo birthdays only three weeks apart, had been Jan's mom's closest friend for almost fourteen years, until events led to a rift several years ago that resulted in a lasting blow to the friendship… and now this. A very painful thought passed through her mind, that now she will never be able to get forgiveness from Beverly and regain that friendship both women had treasured for so many years. Beverly was a good woman… a very good woman… and didn't deserve to suffer Carl's and Maggie's indiscretion. It was strictly alcohol and pot-induced, meant very little to either of them, and yet inflicted a wound on Beverly that would never heal. Maggie had been struggling with guilt and regret ever since. Had she known about Beverly's wild goings on with Marty Dobson, Troy's older brother, and Willard Notch's only judo instructor, she might have been easier on herself. Since Eunice Dobson's older son had absolutely no intention of ever telling anyone out of fear someone would tell his wife, Claire, the secret would be forever buried with Beverly under the "Beloved Wife of Carl" marker right next to Carl's.

"Jan, honey, why don't you lie down for a while. I'll wake you before Troy gets here if you fall asleep."

Jan, in almost robot-like fashion, headed upstairs to her bedroom. She let out a squeal of delight. "Lebowski," where have you been, you poor baby." She pulled the big fur ball off her bed and hugged him close to her chest. And then she burst into tears.

"If only you could talk."

Lebowski Poschner purred loudly in Jan's arms.

Chapter 6

Troy Dobson

Troy Dobson sat in Bessie's Diner on one of those wobbly counter seats that Bessie Darling probably bought fifty years ago, seats begging for replacement. The coffee he was sipping on had that bottom-of-the pot burnt taste… the pursed lipped squint after each sip was a lot like he would do when sipping 100 proof Scotch. His mind was sorting through the few facts he already had from Al Fenton's initial forensic examination of the crime scene, and from his interview with Maggie Hartley. He knew that his interview with Jan would be his only real hope of getting information that could help him track down whoever killed the Poschners. Al had already declared the crime scene as bewilderingly free of the type of forensic data that can make an investigation relatively easy. But not this one. Troy knew he had his work cut out for him on this case, and with the Poschners as popular as they were in the Notch, there would be a lot of pressure on him to solve it quickly. Area residents were not used to being fearful of such things, since all of Menard County had the second lowest violent crime rate in the State, and they expected him to keep it that way. Al had said a few important tests were being run, and maybe he'd get some help from them.

A glance at his black faced Movado watch, a Christmas present from his wife, April, told him it was time to head back to the Poschner home for his interview with Jan. She struck him as a good kid, not at all suspicious looking, but also not a very promising witness with her being in shock and all.

On his way to the Poschners he noticed the high school football team was practicing, probably for its big upcoming game with Mountain Academy. The Jags were pretty good this year, having their best year since the Larry Boynton years, who himself had the Jaguars' best years since, yes, the Troy Dobson years. He had led them to the only State football championship in the school's history, and he was still sort of a big man on campus with the kids. When April was mad at him or just felt like teasing him, she would tell him to get out and go find a sweet little cheerleader who loves to give blow jobs. Over their years together there were several times he gave it a little thought, but he knew April would kill him if he did. Besides, he was very in love with and fully satisfied by his lovely wife, the most beautiful woman in—

He caught himself for a moment, flashing to an image of that gorgeous Ashley Seznicky kid he had noticed at a few games.

So okay, April is the second most beautiful woman in the County. Thinking of her made him want to pop into the house and give her a quick kiss, so he did a quick U-turn and was at his house in a matter of minutes.

April was in the kitchen, and was soon cooing as her handsome manly husband was behind her, arms wrapped around her, kissing and nuzzling the back of her neck the way she loved. The green eyed, full lipped blond with the high cheekbones and flowing long golden hair turned, and lifted her face to him, eyes wide open, and received a passionate kiss from her hunky husband.

"How's your day been?" she asked while still in his arms.

"Well, do you know what happened this morning?"

"You mean about the Poschners?" Troy nodded yes. "Yeah, I heard about it at the Post Office ,: April explained. "Carl was supposed to be at a Zoning Board meeting, and they called his house, and I guess Maggie Hartley was there, really upset about what happened. Pretty shocking, huh?"

"You might say that."

Troy tended to get a little reticent about his work when there was a crisis going on.

"What's Maggie looking like these days?" she asked. " Jesus, I still find it hard to imagine her and Carl getting it on. And then my god, Marty. Marty banging Beverly. Willard Notch sure has a lot of Peyton Place in it !"

April's reference to that 60's novel and movie about an infidelity-riddled small New Hampshire town made Troy chuckle, but only for a moment, as he quickly realized his wife had just given him his first theory about why the murders may have happened.

* * *

Jan 's eyes were swollen from all the crying she had been doing while trying to rest in her bed, with Lebowski cuddled next to her legs. Now she was sitting on the rust colored sofa in the living room, a blanket wrapped around her shoulders and Lebowski on her lap. She was sipping her favorite whiskey, George Dickel Tennessee Sour Mash Bourbon, much mellower, she believed than all those Kentucky Straight bourbons, and likely to have a desperately needed numbing effect on her.

Troy was trying to go easy with her, and yet felt he needed to get every bit of information from her that he could, since she was his only real source. He knew it was tough on her to have to repeatedly search her mind for the details of a traumatic event she so badly wanted to forget… but it was what he had to do.

"Sheriff Dobson?"

"Call me Troy," he interrupted.

"Troy, my mind just isn't working right now. Can we do this tomorrow?"

"Jan, I would love to do this at a better time for you. You deserve that. But I need to file a murder report on the same day it happens."

"When will the forensic autopsy be done?" Jan was obviously showing off her TV crime scene knowledge.

"I'll probably hear late tonight, and I'll swing by in the morning to discuss it with you."

"Okay, but not too early. I feel like I could sleep for a week. Okay, so what do you need from me now?"

Jan was baffled by the questions he asked about Lebowski, almost as though her lovable cat was a possible suspect, but she was too tired to ask about it. She just answered his questions for another half hour, and then mumbled a "Thank you, Jesus" to herself when Troy got up to leave.

"See you in the morning, Jan, and I'm really very sorry for your terrible loss."

"Yup, see you tomorrow, and thank you."

Troy responded with a simple "Yup," and headed home to April. Thinking about Carl and Beverly Poschner, he decided to hold her extra close in bed that night.

Chapter 7

Larry Boynton

Larry Boynton was laying back in his bed, head against the two pillows propped against the maple headboard of his full size bed, joint in hand, and talking into the phone that was lying on his stomach. He had just received the anticipated call from Ashley, smiling to himself about how right he had been about something big going on between the two of them the night before.

She sounded nervous when she started with the "Hi, Larry…it's Ashley…Ashley Seznicki." They both chuckled when he said it was good she told him Seznicki, because otherwise he might have thought it was a different Ashley. A brief silence followed, but it was clear that both were caught up with some mutual feelings that needed no verbal expression. Larry also was becoming aware that a bulge was developing in his white briefs, which was all he was wearing.

"What were you doing when I called?" she asked quite innocently.

Even though he had just been smoking some weed and thinking about her, he did that typical guy thing of saying, "You don't really want to ask that," oozing with sexual innuendo.

"No, really," she said, sounding slightly annoyed, but also emitting a slight giggle. Women, he thought, always with mixed feelings about "guy stuff," disdainful but drawn, all at the same time.

"No, I was just kidding. What I really was doing was lying in bed, smokin' a joint, and thinking about Ashley. Beautiful Ashley."

Her voice softened as she asked, "Were you really?"

His voice softened as he replied, "Yes."

Again, some silence followed, but each became aware of the other's breathing.

Larry broke the emotionally meaningful silence with, "So what are you up to, this lovely morning, lovely lady?"

"Wow, dude, you really lay it on, don't you!"

"Should I stop?"

"No, definitely not," and with that, they both giggled.

Larry's thoughts to himself were about how much he really liked this girl… a whole lot. The only time he ever thought he was in love was about seven years ago. It was with a black-haired, dark eyed, hot bodied woman he couldn't stop thinking about for many months after he saw her. Unfortunately, she was already married to some dude named Badem, lived in both California and Spain, and the only way he could ever get to spend time with his beloved was to watch one of her movies… which he frequently did. It took a long time for him to get past his first and only "love affair," and he could still feel one of those "bulges" when he would fantasize about her… but those times with Penelope Cruz were pretty infrequent these days. However, in spite of all the women he had attempted a relationship with or just banged, he had never re-captured that in-love feeling. Most of the girls he had sex with were so hot for him that he felt as though he had no chance to develop his own feelings for them. The closest to it was Larissa, the girl from Benton that he had dated for a year. She was a really sweet girl, and he did like her a lot, and her being black made things easier, but he didn't experience real passion with her, certainly not the kind of passion he could have experienced with Penelope, if only he had the chance, or, with Ashley Seznicki last night.

"Oh shit, listen, Babe, I just realized I'm working today from noon to eight, and I've got to get going, but can I call you tonight?"

"Of course you can, but ," she asked, "did you just call me Babe?"

"Huh? Oh my god, yeah, I did. Pretty weird, huh? I guess I just feel very comfortable with you."

"And connected?" Ashley asked, in almost a whisper.

Larry paused for a moment, and became keenly aware of his expanding bulge, and then in an equally whispery voice, "Yeah. I do. A lot."

There was just silence for a few moments, and then Ashley said, "I'll let you go, but please call me tonight, okay?"

"I will, Ashley. Ashley, I—"

"Go to work!" she interjected.

"Yes, Ma'am," he responded, and they laughed as they disconnected their call.

* * *

Larry had been flipping burgers after high school, but within six months he had gotten that lucky phone call from Sam Kendall, the owner of the area's largest General Motors dealership, telling him how much he admired Larry for his football exploits (Sam had played for the Jags many years before Troy Dobson, but never had the success Willard Notch's two sports icons had), and that he wanted him to work as a salesman for Kendall Motors. Sam knew the public relations bonanza Larry would bring to the dealership, being a sports hero and an African American, and ever since that phone call, Larry had been proving Sam right, enjoying the job, and being appropriately compensated. He appeared in most of the TV ads, and was the unofficial face of the dealership ("Much sexier than good ol' Sam," the women working there would say).

"Hi, Sam."

"My main man, Larry. How's it goin'?"

"Great, thanks. How's the day going so far?"

It was one of the two days each week that Sam kept the dealership open in the evening, and it was Larry's turn to stay until eight, and close up shop. He was in rotation with two other sales people to be evening manager. One was Archie Rambeault, an old time New Hampshirite with that delightful accent that charmed the pants off prospective car buyers, and he also got them to believe he was honest, making them feel safe. The other was Marge Thromeyer, a very beautiful blond where the joke among the men was that if you were lucky enough to have Thromeyer throw one your way, you'd never forget it. While she was supposedly happily married to a much older bank president, Larry had to repeatedly reject her sometimes downright lewd attempts to seduce him.

"No way, Jose!" was how Larry always reacted to what he considered to be her dangerous attempts to mess up his career by getting the dealership's young black guy to ball the white Assistant Manager, wife of the prominent Charles W. Thromeyer, and the not-so-secret mistress of his boss.

"Hey, listen Larry, my man." (Sam and Larry once had a discussion about the difference for African American men between the words man and boy, and Sam had ever since been on the correct side of that issue.) "When you close tonight, please make sure you leave enough food in the shack for Ken and Dall. Archie didn't leave them enough the other night, and they were hungry and crazy enough to scare the hell out of me when I opened in the morning."

"Will do," Larry assured.

Ken and Dall were two menacing and potentially deadly pit bulls who roamed and patrolled the vast fenced in premium car parking lot at night. Filled with BMWs, Porsches, Lamborghinis, Jaguars, and even a few Mercedes, it had been a pet project of Sam Kendall's for years. He sometimes turned a pretty penny, as they say, selling them. Like the other day when he sold a black Jag to that creepy stranger. It had been Sarah Kendall's idea to name them Ken and Dall as a play on the family name, and Sam always did what Sarah wanted…except stay away from that slutty Marge Thromeyer. Larry, like the others who worked there, hated those dogs, but it was part of their job, and all in all, Kendall Motors was a great place to work.

The evening dragged by rather slowly, with only two customers, both of whom just wanted to look around. The early darkness and wet leaves made for a lousy night to walk through the lots, and such conditions did tend to keep people away.

Larry's eagerness to call Ashley was no longer an issue, as she had call him shortly after he first got to work to tell him about the horrifying call she got from Jan about her parents' murders, and that she would be spending the whole day and overnight at the Poshner house to be there for Jan. Larry told her he didn't really know the Poschners but to please express his condolences to Jan, and he offered to be with her whenever the funeral was going to be.

At eight o'clock Larry told the other employees there for the evening shift to head home, and he proceeded through the steps involved in closing up the dealership. There were certain doors to be locked, and lights, except for those in the glitzy showroom, to be shut off. When he got out into the cold and damp night air he felt chilled, and the thin sliver of moon that showed threw no mellowing light at all.

He glanced over at the pre-fab shack in a back corner of the lot with the super cars, and muttered, "Okay, you ugly little devils, here I come."

He actually hated pit bulls, but did his duty with Ken and Dall very carefully for the sake of Sam and Sarah, who considered the monsters their grandchildren. Their only child, their son Peirson, was severely injured in the Gulf War, and was highly unlikely to ever have kids. As Larry walked toward the shack he started talking to "the boys," as Sarah often called them… "Hey, Ken, hey, Dall. I'm coming, you guys, and I'm going to give you food. Yes, I said FOOD!"

The wet leaves were unusually slippery, and Larry had to use his raised arms for balance like a high wire performer to get to the shack without falling. He wondered if the boys were sleeping, because ordinarily they'd be yelping by now.

All was eerily quiet as he got to the door and unlocked the padlock dangling from the door handle. "C'mon you guys, let's get going," he said, as he swung the door open… but just more silence from within. It was too dark for Larry to see into the dank interior, and he wished he has brought that yellow utility flashlight that Sam kept behind the main service desk. The smell emanating from inside was unusually disgusting, he thought, but more importantly, where were Ken and Dall?

The situation reminded Larry of when he was a kid, living for a while at Grandpa Stubbs's farm in northern Virginia, and often being the lucky one who got to clean the chicken shit, as they liked to call it, out of the chicken coop. He often wondered why he was luckier more often than his cousins Anthony and Aldis, who were fraternal twins, and looked very little like each other except for their very dark skin. The two would often be laughing at Larry as he'd be trudging off to the coop with shovel and pail in hand. And it was on those mornings that he typically skipped breakfast. He and his mom and his older sister, Roberta, lived there for almost two years when he was seven. Unfortunately, Roberta only lived there for a little over a year, when she drowned at age nine, swept away in the Cotton River, made swollen and dangerously rapid by three consecutive days of heavy rain. The horror of it all made their second year there a very dark and depressing one.

His mom, who had had Roberta slip out of her hand as they tried to get into grandpa's old wooden row boat, never forgave herself for letting go of her young daughter, even though two other tragedies of that same type had happened in Hanson's Grove that day.

His mother was there with him that second year, but for Larry she was emotionally absent, and It was during that year, he believed, that he had learned to be very independent, right up to today.

He and his mom moved up to Willard Notch the year after that at the urging of Auntie Bea, his mom's older sister, who lived in nearby Wingset. The only times he ever saw his dad during those years was at Roberta's funeral and one time in Santa's Village in Jackson. That visit was by special arrangement with Virginia's Blossom County Court after his dad was discharged from jail, having been serving time for possession of heroin. He seemed to be a really nice guy, but with no capacity to be an active father for his son. So Larry, essentially, brought himself up. He was always a good kid, never broke a law, and avoided getting into fights even though he could definitely take any of the boys in High School. At UNH, there were some incredibly strong big guys, especially on the Wildcats football team, but he would never fight a teammate. Guys really liked Larry a lot, unless they were racist bigots or if he had messed with someone's girlfriend. He had his share of both.

Now he was in a pitch dark foul-smelling shack, and not very happy about it. He heard a rustling sound behind him, and turned just quickly enough to get a split second look at the two piercing eyes penetrating his soul like lasers. And then he was on the ground, bleeding out from major incisions along his torso and one big one around his neck. He thought he heard a cheering stadium crowd as darkness closed in and his breathing was permanently halted.

In the distance was the sound of some barking dogs. Otherwise, all was quiet at Kendall Motors.

Chapter 8

More Pieces to the Puzzle

Ashley had rushed to the Poschner's house as soon as she got Jan's call. They were both now sipping tea as Jan spilled out more events of the day, more memories of her parents, and more tears.

"Who could possibly do such a thing?" Ashley pondered out loud.

"I don't know," Jan whimpered, breaking into tears. "It had to be someone who really hated them. Or me."

* * *

"Shut the Christ up, you stupid bitch," Ted McGinnis crooned to his wife, Mary, who looked at least ten years older than her forty-two years... It wasn't easy living with Willard Notch's most abusive husband. She actually feared for her life at times when he had been drinking extra heavily... and the smell of his sweat, foul tooth decay, and Captain Morgan's Spiced Rum was sometimes enough to make her want to puke. But, she never did... she always was able to fight off the urge, motivated by the fear of a broken nose or lost teeth. Ted would definitely be pissed off if she ever puked on the kitchen floor he demanded she always keep clean and shiny. Tonight he was drunk, and tonight she was scared, and tonight was like most of their nights.

Mary Marie Hardesty, a very pretty eighteen year old, had met Theodore William McGinnis, a twenty-four year old cab driver, when both were living in Manchester. She had just started community college, planning to work in data processing, and he, when not getting drunk with his friends and/or getting laid, had no plans at all. But when young, sweet, vulnerable Mary Marie Hardesty got into his taxi by herself that snowy February day, he started planning. Before they got to the off-campus apartment she shared with two other girls, Ted had figured out a few things, such as that she definitely was attracted to what many women told him was his "bad boy" aura, that she was not very close to her widowed mother (Mary always referred to her mother, Sue Hardesty, as widowed to cover for the absence of any father in her life) who lived over in Cookman, that she liked ice skating, and while in no way a beautiful girl, was "built like a brick shit house," all in her favor.

Several dates, including one for ice skating (Ted had played hockey in high school), and Mary was eating out of his hand, as he liked to brag to his friends. She was very good to him, often cooked for him, and followed directions sexually pretty well, except for her occasional prudish streak, which he was able to handle with careful use of the term "icy bitch."

After about six months came the day she sheepishly told him she was pregnant. He couldn't help busting her lips, but did nothing mean below her neck, because he was not going to be a baby killer, as appealing as the idea was : that kind of trouble he didn't need.

She said if he needed her to, she would go back home and have the baby there, and never bother him again. His first response was, "Good! And don't fuckin' come around when the kid is older, lookin' for help," but after she was gone for about ten days, and after he had almost been shot by an angry Gulf War veteran husband whose wife he had messed with, he had a quick change of heart, went to Willard Notch where she was temporarily living with a cousin, told her he loved her, moved in, got married, and soon had a baby boy they named Billy.

Mary was very happy after Billy's birth…for about three weeks, which is when she found out from her tearful cousin that Ted had come into her room the night before, obviously drunk, and stuck his hand under her nightgown. His respect and admiration for Mary's cousin, Kathleen, ended rather abruptly when Mary confronted him, and he declared they shouldn't be living with such a sick bitch anyway, and a week later the three of them were living in their own apartment.

The years that followed were very rocky, to say the least, with many job problems and losses and infidelities from Ted, and many bumps, bruises, and a few breaks for Mary, as well as a few menial jobs to keep food on their table (and Captain Morgan's in the liquor cabinet). She had dropped out of her college program when she got pregnant, and still only dreamed of having a real career. Billy got some bumps and a few bruises himself from his dad, but when Ted was drunk it was Mary he focused on. When Billy left home after high school by enlisting in the Coast Guard, Mary was relieved, glad he escaped, and felt a big step closer to escaping, too. But several years ago Ted got wind of her intention to leave him, and he put her into the Menard County General Hospital for five days with a broken nose and fractured pelvis, the result of an unfortunate fall down the basement stairs, she had told the emergency room admissions person. Ted had also told her he would kill her if she ever tried to leave, and she always paid careful attention to Ted's declaration… because she knew he meant it. When Billy called and said maybe he'd come in from San Diego that Christmas, Mary lied, and told him they were going to be away (they never went away), and he should think about next Christmas. She missed her only child terribly, and it broke her heart to do that, but better a broken heart than a broken neck for either of them.

April Dobson awoke to the lovely feeling of Troy's arms clos-ing around her and his face nuzzled into the back of her neck. So warm, so safe, the blanket covering all but the tops of their heads. It was all so blissful, although her still half-asleep brain told her something was oddly different. She said nothing, but concentrated on the feelings and sensations of the moment un-til she could identify what it was. Troy was noticeably anxious, not in that "I'm worrying you won't want to turn so I can get inside you" way she had grown to quickly recognize and often want to quietly and lovingly alleviate, but in a different way. A scared way?

"Troy, Honey, what's wrong?"

"Huh? Oh, nothing, Sweetie. Nothing."

She let a minute pass, and then, "Troy Arthur Dobson, talk to me!" in a whispered but firm voice. She only used the middle name he had abandoned years ago when she needed emphasis with him. As usual, her "command" was his command.

"I don't know, Hon, that Poschner thing has me a little rattled, I guess."

April pondered his response, and offered, "Troy, anyone would be having a hard time with that, I suppose, but I've never seen you shaken like this before. Why? What's going on, babe?"

"I don't know. There was something about that scene in their bedroom that felt kind of creepy... weird, and I think Al felt it, too."

"Did he come up with anything strange?"

"No, at least not yet. He said he was going to run a few tests and call me tomorrow. It's like I think there may be more com-ing, you know, serial killer stuff."

"Oh god," yelled April, "it will be panic time in good old Willard Notch!"

"Yeah, I know," Troy responded softly. "If there's another one like this one the whole town will go nuts."

April pulled Troy on top of her, saying, "C'mon, cowboy, let's squeeze one in while we still can."

They both laughed, but just for a second, as they began to seriously engage in their soul-consuming process of squeezing one in.

* * *

Rob and Ed Zanermann sat at the dining room table with all lights off except for the small floral stain glass lamp on the old 1960's credenza that housed all the family videos made over the years before Marsha broke everyone's hear. No videos had ever been made since then, and even plain photos were at a minimum. They had been sitting together in silence for a full ten minutes, something that had never before happened in the Zanermann household.

Both had a rather glassy- eyed look, or maybe dazed being the better word, and the lack of talk seemed more like an "I can't" rather than an "I don't want to" in both of them.

"Long day," said Ed, breaking the long silence.

"Mmm," Rob responded.

"You okay?"

"Mmm," was again Rob's response.

"I've decided not to work today. I'm not going to open the store. Fuck the store!"

His dad's use of an f-bomb startled Rob out of his daze. Ed Zanermann was never much for profanity.

"Really?"

"Yeah, really," Ed growled. "Fuck it!"

More silence. Then Rob got out of his chair, went over to where his father sat and bent down enough so that he could look squarely into his eyes, something they, and so many other fathers and sons rarely ever did, maybe because of Oedipal fear fantasies, as Freud had thought, or maybe because of male intimacy fears, which Rob knew, and as Jan frequently reminded him, all too well.

"Oh shit!" he bellowed. "You, too?"

"Me, too, what?" Ed barked.

"You met him, too. You met him, too!"

Rob seemed frantic... Ed stared at Rob for a full minute, and then muttered, "Go to bed."

* * *

Lebowski was already in bed, waiting for Jan to join him. Occasionally he would drift off, curled in a tight ball, and purring loudly. He would wake up for a moment and lift his head whenever he thought he heard sounds that meant she was on her way up, and then doze off again when it appeared she wasn't. Soft voices from downstairs were signifying Jan was saying goodnight to her friend, Ashley, none of which Lebowski was awake for, and none of which would have affected him at all even if he had been. But then came a sound that jerked Lebowski awake. He bolted upright, jumped off the bed, and then scooted under it. The sound was simply the closing of a car door, followed by a very slight growling sound, perceptible only to a cat's ears.

* * *

All hell seemed to break loose in the morning when Sam Kendall opened up the Dealership and found both Ken and Dall in the shed, plopped down on a very bloody floor next to the carved up (and slightly chewed) body of Larry Boynton. By the time Al Fenton, Troy Dobson and Deputy Sheriff Eddie Anton arrived on the scene, word of the second bestial crime in Willard Notch in less than twenty-four hours had spread pretty much throughout the downtown area. Conjecture as to who could have committed two such heinous crimes ran the gamut, including from

Bubbie Zanermann, who concluded from her nursing home bed that it was those god-awful pit bulls.

Part II

XS AND YS

Chapter 9

Al

Al Fenton was sucking on a long black Dominican cigar and listening to a CD of the Three Tenors. He was in the forensics laboratory room of the Menard County Courthouse and Jail building. While it was actually a sizable and well laid out lab for a small time operation like theirs, it was indeed not exactly equipped to modern standards, and Al at times had to be very creative in order to be able to offer the Sheriff's office some valuable help. Many times he just wasn't able to. Because he was such a good natured guy and gave his all to the job, he had outlasted everyone's longevity predictions when he first started. While Sheriff Dobson sometimes wished for someone more sophisticated, he really liked Al, and seemed content to rely on his brand of forensics. no matter how limited it might be at times.

Albert Louis Fenton was fifty-seven, married for twenty-six years to Kay Bradley, his high school sweetheart, who had passed twelve years ago due to breast cancer. She had given up one breast in an attempt to beat that devil, but two years later the other breast was gone, and six months after that, so was she. They never did have kids, since she had a congenital problem with her uterus, but they were Auntie Kay and Uncle Al to seven kids from their combined siblings. They loved those roles as a variation on the "you can love and enjoy them without having to be responsible for their well-being" theme that grandparents often spoke of. One thing Al was always sure of was that he missed that woman something awful right up to today. In all the years since her death, he had had exactly one date, forced on him by a well-meaning brother and sister-in-law, just enough to validate his feeling that there could never ever be a replacement for his Kay.

Al only had one picture of Kay in his lab, but he had them everywhere at home. She was a willowy brunette who was an inch taller than Al, and her slender build offset his plumpness quite nicely. They used to joke that if she was also plump, they'd probably have some trouble with sex; as they were, it was a good fit. He smiled... god, he loved that woman so much, and he always got a warm, proud feeling about himself when he recollected how respectful and caring he had always been toward her... unlike some other notorious husbands in Willard Notch, especially Ted McGinnis. He was just a total asshole when it came to how he treated his wife, Mary, who herself was a really nice person, better than Ted could ever hope to be. How in the world so many nice women ended up with real assholes like Ted he just couldn't fathom. He and Kay had once seen a movie about spousal abuse, with Farrah Fawcett, when Kay explained to him afterwards that women are often stuck in such relationships because of fear... fear of male anger and rage. Al had a little trouble understanding her at first, because he was himself a very gentle man, just like his dad and granddad before him. Kay got her point across by revealing to him an incident when she had briefly been afraid of him, something she had never felt a need to tell him about. He was shocked to hear her tell of a time when they were having an argument about some minor issue, and he in his frustration with her had pounded his fist on the arm of his recliner to emphasize the point he was trying to make. He had started to assure her that the gesture was just a gesture, not a real anger thing, and she told him to relax, that she knew that afterwards, but that she reacted in a startled way because she grew up watching her father actually use that "gesture" a lot to intimidate her mother, and once actually did hit her. Well, that was a lesson from his sweetheart he never forgot, that male anger could be a very scary thing for a female. But when the asshole was as bad as Ted McGinnis, he still wondered why Mary stayed.

And, it was no small coincidence that he was thinking about all this as he again turned his attention from the corpse of Carl Poschner to that of Beverly. He had already noted that there was clearly a difference between the degrees to which each had been carved up, with Beverly's wounds significantly more severe, but he was even again taken aback by the extra savagery evident on her body. The biggest difference was that while her face was really like sliced Wonder Bread, Carl's was essentially untouched.

This extra goody for Beverly had made him especially anxious to get the results of her DNA testing back from Manchester where they'd be checking for sexual assault evidence… or maybe just more animus toward her.

For a moment Al pondered why his thoughts were running toward Ted McGinnis, Farrah Fawcett, and animus, but his cigar was beginning to taste like Brutus's poop, Brutus being the Pug he had gotten for companionship not long after Kay's passing., and he turned his attention to the toilet adjoining his lab for disposal. How did he know what Brutus's poop tastes like? That involved a story he vowed to himself never to tell.

As he was about to return to the Poschners, his phone vibrated in his pocket. He hated the ringing of phones ever since he got the call about Kay while he had been doing an emergency examination on a pretty 17-year-old jogger raped and murdered in Sunday Park, and it happened on a Sunday. Let's just say it was a bad day all around, and one that Al to this day considered the worst one of his life.

He was hoping it was Manchester's forensic lab calling, but no such luck. H e was hoping maybe the "Rush" order attached to the evidence would speed them up, but he knew all too well that even with that order it would be close to a week before anything conclusive could be available. Without the order? Probably a couple of months. The word was that Manchester was backed up worse than ever.

When it turned out to be April Dobson, he was disappointed, but glad to talk to April, who was a hell of a good kid. From the time they first met, she had made sure she and Troy had him over for dinner at least once a month, and man, could that woman cook. Her good old fashioned baked Finnan Haddie was the best he had ever had since that of his blessed mother who had grown up in Scotland.

April was calling to tell him Troy got a late start but would be at the lab soon. She said he was hoping Al would wait for him, and maybe even have some findings for him.

Al chuckled, and said, "April, Honey, I'll certainly wait for him, but findings ? I'm afraid we'll be waiting a while for that."

"Okay, Al. Hey, what are you doing for dinner Friday? You know that's fish night in the Dobson household."

"I think I'm dining at the Dobson's?"

It was April's turn to chuckle. "See you at 6:30, Al."

Al returned to Beverly Poschner's corpse, and was just starting to take a closer look at her knife wounds when his phone rang again. This time it was Troy, saying, "Al, get down to Kendall Motors right away. We've got another one. I just got a call from Sam."

"See you there," Al replied, and immediately headed out. He hadn't even to take the time to say another what?

Another murder? My god, Willard Notch was not exactly a Chicago, U. S. A., so maybe it was auto theft, but the urgency in the Menard County Sheriff's voice told him it was more likely the former than the latter.

Chapter 10

Troy, Al, and Larry

"Holy shit, Troy. We got a serial killer in the Notch, don't we?"

"Yeah, you might say that, Al." Troy was still reacting to hearing Al swear for the first time, maybe ever. Al was not the type to curse… too respectful of just about everything, but especially God. "We got a lot of work ahead of us, Al. Maybe I can get April to cook us up some dinner and bring it over later."

"Sounds good to me, Troy. That wife of yours is the best cook in at least Northern New England."

Al did a cursory examination of the gruesome crime scene, repeatedly muttering to himself, "Poor kid." Several of Troy's assistants were starting to get the bloody corpse of Larry Boynton ready for transportation to Al's lab, and Troy was interrogating Sam Kendall about what had happened at the lot last night and then his discovery this morning, and also getting DNA samples from Ken and Dall, both of whom were unusually subdued.

As they were getting ready to leave, Marge Thromeyer sidled up to Troy, put a hand on his shoulder, and said with a slight, phony Southern accent, "Why Sheriff Dobson, aren't you going to interview me?" When he told her no, at least not for now, she threw in a comment oozing with innuendo. "Well, you know how to find me when you're ready."

Troy totally ignored the pitch Thromeyer threw, and hopped into his shiny new beige and black cruiser (new colors chosen by the Town Council in May), although he did turn back for a quick glance at the Town's hottest female as he pulled out of the lot.

* * *

Now back at the Menard County Forensics Lab, Al and Troy were sitting next to the metal table on which Larry Boynton, or what was left of him, was stretched out. The damage done to this young man's body was more extensive than either of them had realized back at Kendall's.

"Troy," Al asked, " do you think we need to bring in the FBI ?"

"Let's wait to see what happens with Manchester when they get all your stuff."

"Yeah, okay, but this sure is pretty gruesome, isn't it?"

"Al, my man, I get the feeling you are scared shitless."

"Yes, Troy. Aren't you?"

"Scared, no, but I am really worried about how the Town is going to handle it. I think we need to have an agreed upon way of talking about it all, and we should meet with Charlie Fogg about how they should write things up in tomorrow's Notch Ledger and Menard County Tribune. We need to review everything, including obituaries, before they print. We don't want to create panic."

Al lit up one of his Dominican "black beauties," as Troy called them, and began a closer examination of Larry's body. Some half-formed thought was nagging at him... If only he could grab onto whatever it was. Troy was continuing to write his report from the morning, disrupted just for a few seconds when an image of Marge Thromeyer's protruding nipples flashed through his mind... But he was disciplined enough to push it away and continue the report.

"Troy!" Al shouted to the County Sheriff, who sat not more than ten feet from him. "Troy, look at this! Oh my god. Why didn't I see this before!"

"What are you ranting about, Al?"

"Look at the cuts all over his body. I'm pretty sure no knife did those!"

"Why?"

"We've got to look at Boynton's cuts and at the Poschners cuts as identical, and they are much too uniform and evenly spread in clusters to be from a knife... The guy would have to spend hours being this precise with a blade, and both of these murders were pretty obviously violently passionate, and not committed methodically."

"So what do you think we're dealing with?"

"Damned if I know! Well, that's not really true. I do have a theory, sort of, but I'm embarrassed to say it. Oh, hell, I think it could have been an animal rather than a person. It looks like there were big swipes with a paw with evenly spread out claws. Christ, Troy. I don't know."

Troy was immediately struck by the possibility of Al's theory being correct. And his thoughts went immediately to Ken and Dall. So subdued at the crime scene, and pretty good evidence that they were the ones eating Larry in the shed, what with a small piece of Larry's shirt fabric blood stuck to Dall's jowl. Troy never did like those dogs.

In fact, the whole town took a dim view of the "Viciousness Twins," as they were called by many Notch citizens.

"Ken and Dall?" Troy asked. "Well, sure as shootin', they were right there! But it looks like the same animal, if it was an animal, did all three killings. What would the other one be doing while that was happening? Wait, how could they have gone to the Poschner home the night before to kill Carl and Beverly and then be back in the lot the next morning, according to Sam?"

"Yeah, that's right. I think maybe I should go back to Kendall's and question Sam some more."

" Troy, d o you think Sam might have had something to do with it? Like, did he have something against Carl and Beverly?"

"I don't know, Al… I doubt it, but we can't rule out anything at this point."

"Yeah, but what would he have against Larry? He always talked about the kid like he was a son."

"I don't know," Troy winked back at Al, "but I'm going to talk to Marge again, too."

Al seemed to get Troy's point immediately, and simply said, "Watch out for that one. She's dangerous to your health."

Troy just smiled as he went out the door, and within a quick minute was on his way back to Kendall Motors.

Al went over to Larry's shredded body, looking at the kid's handsome caramel colored face. Al typically never looked a corpse in the eye like he was now doing. His eyes actually misted over as he made note of what a sweet kid Larry had always seemed to be.

"God, kid, do I wish you could talk to me right now," he mumbled largely to himself. Force of habit from thousands of conversations in his lifetime made him look at Larry's face for some sign of response. Seeing none, he sighed deeply, and re-lit his partially smoked Dominican Black Beauty.

Chapter 11

Sam, Marge, and Sheriff Dobson

When Troy got back to Sam's lot, Marge was standing outside in front of the showroom, with a customer. It was Ralph Akers, in the process of buying Julie a replacement for the old Chevy she had totaled four days before. Marge waved to Troy as he got out of his vehicle, and he called out to her that he wanted to talk to her, but needed to talk to Sam first, asking if he was in his office. She responded by both saying he was in, and also by giving Troy an alluring smile and wink, conveying that she was all ready for him to do her next. Troy got her drift.

Sam was sitting at his carved walnut antique desk in his otherwise unremarkable office. A dropped ceiling, cheap carpeting, and chrome-framed furniture added a touch of cheapness to the impressive desk, which looked painfully out of place and stylistically overwhelmed in the room. Sam was staring out the window when Troy entered. He turned slowly and asked the Sherriff why he had come back so soon. He described for Troy how riddled he now was with horrible images from discovering the ghastly corpse of that lovely kid, a kid who was his favorite employee. When Troy started asking a few questions about Marge, Sam became visibly less comfortable. It was common knowledge, but never talked about, that he had been balling Marge ever since she came to work for him six years ago, that she was his highest paid employee, and that he and she frequently checked into the Granite State Suites hotel as Jack and Irma Howard for their trysts. Troy knew Sam was very protective of his "secret" mistress, and sometimes had small fits of jealousy regarding attention she'd get from mail customers. Troy very gingerly put that issue on the table, and then asked Sam if he thought she and Larry had ever hooked up. Sam said absolutely not, that Larry was a great kid who was very ethical, and that Marge had once told him that the kid wasn't her type. Sam believed Marge and naively assumed she wouldn't want a black guy, and Troy believed Sam, and that Sam Kendall bore no ill will toward Larry Boynton. Troy knew racism was alive and well in Willard Notch, but not very much in Sam Kendall.

After about five more minutes of conversation, Troy said he needed to ask Marge a few questions and would then be on his way. Sam wished him good luck with the investigation, and Troy was in Marge's office a minute or two after that. "Alone at last," Marge joked, but Troy just started right in with some serious questions designed to ferret out if any troubling issues might have been operating in that potential triangle. Marge, who knew Troy was aware of her clandestine relationship with Sam, was quite open about how Sam, while extremely jealous of almost any man looking at her, definitely including the Menard County Sheriff himself, never expressed any concerns about Larry and her, because he saw the kid as very honorable, as never wanting to endanger his job, and probably with no interest in older white women, no matter how beautiful. She did explain to Troy how ironic that was, because Larry was someone she often had fantasies about having sex with.

Troy just gave Marge a neutral head nod in response to her disclosure about Larry, but then she looked at him with that maddeningly erotic half-smile she often showed him and added, "And I have them about you, too, Troy. All the time."

His response, some of it involuntary, was quite different this time. Her silken blond hair was piled up in a very stylish knot, her full lips were parted and looking ever so moist, and her red silk blouse was unbuttoned down to her cleavage, nipples quite evident through the tight silk veil her blouse provided. She took two steps toward him, he took two toward her, and they were instantly locked in a passionately hungry kiss.

"Oh god, Troy, I want you so bad," she whispered into his ear.

In Troy's head he was screaming, "No! April! Dear god! April, I love you! But dear god, I—!" But he was silent as he backed Marge up to a work table near her desk and hoisted her on to it, opened her up while she was doing the same for him, and plunged himself into that age old mix of instant molten ecstasy followed by searing shame. He started sobbing, and said to Marge, "Marge, I can't," in response to which she smilingly interrupted with, "Troy, honey, you just did."

Chapter 12

April and Troy

April Dobson was putting the finishing touches on one of her fabulous lasagnas, this one lavished with lots of pepperoni in addition to the usual meat sauce. In her experience, going back to when her mother would make it to please her father, it was the version of lasagna that men liked best. She knew that Troy loved it, and she figured that Al probably would, too. She made a fairly large one; knowing the guys were likely to be working late in the Lab, and would probably love a lasagna encore when their stomachs began to gurgle.

She packed up the dish, covering it with both tin foil and towels to keep it extra warm, added a paper bag with a half dozen chocolate chip cookies, and took off for the Menard County Jail and the County Sheriff's Department building, listening to her favorite country music station, which at the moment was playing the Patsy Cline classic "I Go To Pieces." She was soon at the building, and carried her goodies over to the Forensics Lab to show those two sweet men how much she cared for them. She found Al alone, reading a book entitled *The Forces of Nature: The Predators* which he promptly slammed shut when he saw her and simultaneously smelled that incredible *Lasagna a la April*, as he liked to call it.

"Well, looky, looky, it's that beautiful woman carrying a beautiful dinner for two beautiful guys."

"April giggled and responded with an"Absolutely! Hey, Al, where is my not-so-chubby hubby?"

Al put on a mock frown and said, "Are you implying that I—I, Al Fenton—am CHUBBY?"

They both had a good laugh, and then Al mentioned the Kendall Motors business and that Troy should be back very soon.

"Not if that Marge Thromeyer digs her claws into him!" April joked, fully believing that such a thing could never, would never, happen with Troy. Al smiled, slightly uncomfortably, because he knew guys a little better than April, although he himself was quite proud of never having cheated on Kay.

April went on, still smiling, "If he's not back soon, and if it's because of that Thromeyer woman, you tell him he has twenty-four hours to move out, and that I'll be having you move in the next day!"

Al held back on telling April he could sure go for that, because women get offended by dumb guy comments like that, and he had no wish to offend such a nice young woman, and especially his boss's wife.

"Well, Al, I think I 'm going to head out to do a few errands, and then head home. Tell Troy to call me after you guys have eaten to let me know how late he might be."

"Sure thing, April, and thanks again for dinner."

April headed over to the nearby Shell gas station, the one owned by that creepy Mr. McDougald who always smelled like rubber tires and stared down her cleavage gap as best he could. After filling her Civic's tank she stopped at Marcy's Bake Shop to pick up the devil's food birthday cake she had ordered for her Aunt Edna's sixtieth birthday party on Saturday and then headed for home.

When she got in, she sat down to enjoy the small pan of lasagna she had set aside for herself. It really was delicious, and she anticipated hearing soon from Troy about just how much he and Al enjoyed it.

Soon, the nippy Fall night air and that early darkness brought on by the season with a little help from its friend, Daylight Savings Time, commanded April's attention.

Still no call from Troy.

She decided to call the Lab. The phone rang three times before Al picked up and greeted April with, "Hi, April. I got so hungry waiting for Troy that I broke into that incredible lasagna myself. Better than ever, April, sweetheart, better than ever."

"Good, thanks for the review, Al. Is Troy there yet?"

"Not yet, April. That new murder certainly has him working on all cylinders."

"Okay, tell him to call me as soon as he gets in."

"Will do, Chef Dobson."

April waited a full forty-five minutes before finally calling Kendall Motors. She got a recording obviously just recently made. "Hi, this is Sam Kendall, Owner and President of Kendall Motors. We are very sad to say we are currently closed due to the untimely death of a beloved member of the Kendall Motors family. Larry Boynton was a fine young man and respected employee of our dealership, and we will miss him dearly. Please leave your message after the beep, and we will get back to you when we re-open. Thank you."

"Damn," April said to no one in particular. She stood thinking intensely for a moment, and then decided to call Sam. But again, a recording. She left no message, as before, but again began questioning her next step. Should she just wait until he calls, or should she call the Thromeyer's house and see if "Maggie The Cat" was there. She was thinking of the Arthur Miller character in a play she had never read but wow, what a movie! She opted to call the Thromeyers. Charles Thromeyer was known around town as a rich snob whose goals in life were said to be, amassing a huge fortune, holding on to his ultra-hot wife, and making all other men feel small. Troy certainly never had anything good to say about him. He answered April's call, and yelled out for Marge to come to the phone after April told him why she was calling.

She could hear some unintelligible mumbling, then a pause, and then, "Well hi, April darlin, how have you been?"

"Fine," April responded. "Did you see Troy today?"

"I sure did, April. What a sweet man he is, April. He came by the dealership today to question Sam and me about Larry Boynton's murder. Isn't it all awful, what with Carl and Beverly and now that nice Boynton boy? Huh? Oh, I'd say around four-thirty or so. Huh? No, I just assumed he was going back to the Department or home. Yeah, hon, you take care, too."

April felt she was hearing something a little off center in Marge's voice, but she let that thought go, as she was beginning to worry about Troy's whereabouts. She waited a short while longer, feeling very unsettled, and eventually hopped into her car and started driving aimlessly. Something inside her was gnawing at her. Damn, if there's a homicidal maniac serial killer in the Notch, wouldn't her sweet husband (when Marge referred to him as sweet she felt like puking) be out there following leads? Putting himself in harm's way, as people like to say about our front line protectors?

Now, April was feeling her anxiety level slowly rising… but then in an instant she suddenly felt it surging through her and momentarily paralyzing her.

She had just been driving past Birch Street, a dimly lit dead end street, when her eye caught the heart-stopping image of the black and beige vehicle of the Menard County Sheriff's Department, smashed into a large tree at the end of the short street, driver's door hanging wide open, and water still dripping down from the obviously destroyed radiator. April finally broke out of her paralysis long enough to yell out, "Troy! Troy!" but she still seemed frozen in her driver's seat, unable to run out to his car as she so desperately wanted to do … but was also dreading. She could tell something was terribly wrong. She continued to sit in her car, tears rolling down her cheeks, as her horrific dread of what was coming next had a firm grip on her, and would not let go.

Chapter 13

Thanksgiving Night:
Jaguars 5, Sue Hardesty 0

Susan Ann Hardesty was a happy-go-lucky, rosy cheeked Sophomore cheer leader who was modestly good looking, moderately popular, and magnificently grateful to the Lord for the bountiful good life she was living. She and her family spent every Sunday at the Birch Grove Baptist Church, being reminded of how generous and loving was their Lord, Jesus Christ, who asked of them only that they live lives of propriety and virtue. Sue loved the Church and Pastor Wilfong, and was very involved in helping him with the Sunday School, as well as with a variety of fund raising activities. She at times wondered if she might become a pastor herself someday.

While Pastor Wilfong often gave sermons about the rampant immorality spreading among contemporary high school students, Sue Hardesty was herself a paragon of virtue, and prided herself in never having given in to the temptations that ensnared so many of her classmates. She wondered if maybe she was the only remaining virgin in the Sophomore class, but had no interest in pursuing that question. She was simply being who she was meant to be.

Sue was not terribly interested in the boys in her school because it was painfully obvious to her that they had absolutely no interest in "the girl who won't put out." She did have one date with Orin McAdams, a nice kid who was known as a "wonk" by his classmates, but it seems he had made the date with her as part of a bet with teasing bullies that she wouldn't even let him grab her boobs. Orin McAdams lost both the bet and any chance of developing a relationship with a kind, warm, intelligent, fun-loving girl. He was overheard saying to his bully-boy taunters, "Naw, her boobs are probably too ugly anyway."

Such was the way of the world at the only high school in Willard Notch, and with maybe the last remaining sophomore virgin. On the brighter side, the Jaguars were having their best football season in a dozen years, and some were saying they might even contend for the Granite State Championship. This was heady stuff for these boys of the gridiron, and they were the toast of the campus. All the guys wanted to hang out with them, and most the girls were fawning all over them and confiding in each other how much they were willing to put out to get next to them.

Parties spawned freely, smuggled alcohol flowed freely, and many a fair maiden fell freely, in this wonderful world of Willard Notch teens.

As for Sue Hardesty? She, too, was a happy teen, happy with her active church life and Pastor Wilfong's sermons about morality and service to God, with her cheerleading, which was her way to admire the football team from a safe distance, and with her fine academic achievement record that she hoped to carry on to Dartmouth, or Middlebury, or Colby College in Maine.

And then came the triumphant Thanksgiving Day Game with a new old rival, Bishop Calderbank High, a not very good team, with the worst record in the Valley League, one of the weakest leagues in New Hampshire. The two schools had quite a rivalry thirty-five years earlier, but BCH had run afoul with a few of the Granite State High School Association rules, and were placed on a three year probation by the Association. The two schools never tried to resume the rivalry, until now. There had been the traditional Wednesday evening rally the night before the "Turkey Day Classic" as it had been dubbed some years before by a Tribune sports writer, replete with band, cheerleaders, the boys of the gridiron, and about a thousand wildly adoring fans. The gathering was supposed to generate extra enthusiasm in the fan base, and Sue was giving all that her physical energy and vocal chords could give to that end, but it appeared that the teenage kings of the gridiron were already whipped up to a fever pitch. One by one, the team members grabbed the microphone and blurted some largely unintelligible rant to the crowd's delight. Eddie Franco, the starting quarterback mumbled something nasty about the lack of character and dishonesty of the Battling Bishops' ancestors, Niles Perry, Jr., who was already accepted at Yale and was All-League wide receiver talked of integrity, honor, and toughness as though he was a recruiter for the Marine Corps, Ronnie Taylor, the six-three, three hundred ten pound right tackle screamed out, "We're gonna destroy 'em," and then Roscoe Walker, their All-State running back, calmly predicted a 35-7 victory for the "Jumpin' Jaguars," as they sometimes called themselves.

The rally left everyone with energy to burn, and Niles Perry spread the word to some friends that his parents were away sailing in the Bahamas, leaving behind only Niles, and his very cool older brother who had just graduated from Yale. He would be starting med school at Dartmouth next year after a year of working in a bio lab at their dad's drug company, Their dad was a major producer of a variety of prescription drugs, and always had a very full liquor cabinet.

T he group responded with the traditional, "Let's have a party!" And party they did. Arriving at Niles's home, besides the players he was most friendly with, were three cheerleaders, several other cute girls who let's say, knew their way around the team, a few other team members, Niles's brother Roy and his girlfriend Peggy, and Leon, a rather strange twenty-six year old who lived next door to the Perry family. Leon was known to be, ironically, a voracious consumer of prescription drugs, a lot of them produced by Perry Pharmaceuticals.

The three cheerleaders were Debbie Kendall, Martha Olinsky, and Sue Hardesty, the latter very unlikely to ever be at such a party, but was there at the urging of Martha, who secretly had been given twenty dollars by Niles for convincing her to come. Martha was great at shooting down Sue's shyness and moral arguments for not coming to Niles's party, and frequently used the expression, "Nothing bad is going to happen to you if you're there!" Martha didn't fully understand that this Baptist high school sophomore was more afraid that she herself might do something bad. And Martha Olinsky was also wrong about the party.

As the party progressed and Niles's insistence that she not be a "party-pooper" wore her down, Sue became willing to sample some alcohol for only the second time in her life. The first was the night she took a sip of Uncle Van's spiked Christmas eggnog when she was nine. It had been spiked with spiced rum, and she just didn't like the taste. But, Niles, in his infinite wisdom, had chosen his mother's delicious favorite, creme de cocoa and milk, and she unfortunately loved it. Within an hour, Sue was having trouble keeping her balance when she walked, and by the time she walked her way into the bedroom where all their Jaguars jackets were piled on the bed, the room was beginning to spin, and she was unable to get all the jackets off the bed. And when five boys followed her into the bedroom and one at a time got onto the bed with her, she was too disabled to do anything about that either.

Sue never did figure out who it was that eventually drove her home, and remembers only that her father was screaming something at her about the Devil when she fell into a very deep sleep.

Sue never really learned much of anything about that night, and never even tried to. Unfortunately, she never learned anything much the rest of her Sophomore year, and it was late Summer just before her Junior year that she had her baby girl that she named Mary Marie after the Virgin Mary. She, of course, had to quit school. She also had to leave town a year later when Pastor Wilfong was caught trying to exorcise the Devil in Sue in a slightly amoral way.

Her daughter would eventually marry, return to Willard Notch and bear her a grandson who as a kid, was a big Boston Celtics fan.

Her son-in-law was a horrible man, but Sue had very understandably decided many years before that there were probably very few good men in the world, so don't expect to find one. This was a lesson she had made sure she taught Mary Marie.

Chapter 14

Lebowski

Lebowski was aggressively licking his left paw, curled up on the hall floor just outside what used to be Carl and Beverly's master bedroom. Again he heard that car door and low growl off in the distance, and after washing his face with that paw, fell asleep for the night.

A full moon was situated high above Willard Notch, illuminating the leaf covered streets of this small Northern New England town, The people of this town were gripped with fear, and Lebowski might have been the only one to sleep well that night.

Part III

X

Chapter 15

April, Eunice, and Mary

Eunice Dobson was soaked to the skin as she sat on a metal folding chair in a downpour, watching her younger son, Troy, the former handsome Sheriff of Menard County, being laid to rest. Huddled against her on either side were her two daughters-in-law, Claire and April. The casket was closed all through the visiting hours the day before and the funeral itself. Al Fenton had guaranteed that no one would want to see that body the way it now was, including April who had seen it but was still in shock with no memory of it. Now, April was silent, staring glassy-eyed at the casket, no crying sounds, but tears continuing to leak from her eyes and roll slowly but steadily down her cheeks.

Anyone close to the Dobson's were more worried about the young and healthy April than about Eunice, who was not so young, had many ailments, and adored her baby boy. Marty had said he worried April could become suicidal, and kindly volunteered to stick close to her and keep an eye on things. The dual meaning in that escaped everyone… except Claire, who knew her husband well enough to be keeping an eye on him. She had figured out years ago that Marty had an affair with Beverly Poschner, and never trusted him again. She never did tell him she knew, being too afraid of how her Black Belt husband might react to confrontation.

April on several occasions had to state she had no intentions of killing herself in spite of how bleak her life had suddenly become. The horrors of finding her best friend and lover dead, sliced up and covered with blood was one thing, a trauma she knew she would have to live with the rest of her life. But what she didn't know how to deal with was the prospects of an empty house and an empty bed. Her mind had not yet even begun to sort out who could have done this, and why.

Neither had Eunice, who had simply become numb with grief.

Eunice Dobson was the type of woman people sometimes refer to as handsome. All her adult life people would say what a handsome woman she was, not because she looked masculine, but because she had a strong, chiseled good looking face, with high cheekbones, intense blue/green eyes, and kept her hair short but stylish. Not a native New Englander, she moved to New Hampshire after marrying Curt Dobson, the very attractive truck driver she had met while waitressing at Big Benny's Truck Stop Restaurant in her native Poughkeepsie, New York. She was living on her own, having just completed junior college, and was spending a year off from school until hopefully attending University of Massachusetts, a college her Aunt Edna had graduated from and about which Eunice had heard many good things. She thought the state universities in Maine, or Vermont, or New Hampshire would be good back-up choices, but falling in love with Curt shifted her focus to the University of New Hampshire system, and when she accepted Curt's proposal after only a few weeks of knowing him, they moved to Willard Notch after a Justice of the Peace ceremony, where she planned to enroll at UNH.

Someone in Eunice's family, Aunt Rachel, her mother's oldest sister, Eunice thinks, once compiled as much of a family tree as she could when Eunice was in junior high. What emerged was a conclusion that she was twenty-five percent Native American, on her mother's side. Her maternal grandmother was a full blooded Cayuga Indian, an upper New York State tribe that was part of the larger Iroquois Nation. Eunice, on the one hand, always felt proud of that heritage, believing in the essential historical nobility of Native Americans. On the other hand, it was a part of her that lay dormant, with Eunice never feeling clear about how and why to express that to the world. Not even her husband and kids knew, and she always felt a little puzzled about why she had never shared her secret pride. It isn't as though she wanted it to be a secret. She just never seemed to experience what felt like the right time and reason. As for her marriage, Eunice did think Curt would be a good husband and dad, but also was motivated to leave Poughkeepsie because Big Benny Anderson, her boss, was becoming a real problem for her. Benny had grabbed her in the kitchen one night and pulled her into the small office out back. He was getting outrageously close to rape, but a huge Allied moving van noisily pulled into the parking lot, and Eunice was able to get away from all six-foot-five, three hundred pounds of Big Benny. When Eunice told him the next day that if he tried to molest her again, she would tell Mrs. Benny (Louise Anderson), he simply glared at her and told her she'd better think that over if she wanted to keep her job. She never did tell Curt about it, figuring just getting out of disgusting Benny Anderson's disgusting truck stop was her best plan.

Her marriage to Curt had its ups and downs as do most marriages, but they produced two fine sons, and attended church as a family every Sunday, Curt would get sleepy but not violent when drunk, and he only cheated on her twice that she knew.

When he died of lung cancer six years ago, they were basically at peace with each other, and Troy and Martin on good terms with him, although not really close. She knew Curt did love his boys, and that it would break his heart if he ever had to bury either of them. As for her? Burying Troy definitely broke her heart. She cared deeply for both her daughters-in-law, but had a special place in her heart for April, because it was obvious how much love there was between her and her baby boy. She exulted in the fact that April always knew for sure that Troy would never cheat on her, that he was not one of those men who always do.

Now, Martin was another story. He was known to have trouble keeping it in his pants, as they say, and it was on more than one occasion that she had to console a wounded Claire. They never had kids, deciding that dedicating themselves to making their martial arts studio, (Claire handling the business end) the best in New Hampshire was the more important thing for them to do. The Menard Martial Arts Studio was now considered by many to be one of the best in all of Northern New England, and that was as close as Eunice was ever going to get to having a grandchild, along with eleven year old Popeye, Claire and Marty's moody cat. But it wasn't that ever-present wish for a grandchild she was feeling now. It was the horror of knowing her baby was ripped to pieces like that.

Who could possibly have had that much hatred and rage toward him? Everyone in Menard County liked him and was glad he was Sheriff. Why, in his last election, he got eighty-three percent of the vote, and rumor was that his opponent, Tom Sheffield voted for Troy because he knew he'd be a better sheriff. Old Tom himself joked that it was good Troy won, because if he himself had won, saying, "Sheriff Sheffield" was like having a mouth full of shit.

That last thought made her chuckle for a moment, causing Claire to turn her head to look with puzzlement at her mother-in-law.

Eunice was momentarily embarrassed, but it quickly passed, and she became aware of how April's still steady flow of tears had created a wet spot on her black pant-suited right thigh. She gave April a hug, and returned to wondering who could have ravaged her son that way.

* * *

Al was back in his lab, now, following the large gathering at Marty and Claire's house. Many people had come, even in the heavy downpour, to pay their respects to April and Eunice, who seemed to be hanging very close to each other all afternoon. Al had decided to leave when he could see that April was totally spent, exhausted from receiving the steady flow of people expressing sympathy and condolences and wanting to give her a hug. He knew she hadn't eaten a thing except for one of Helen Shaw's brownies that she wolfed down with some coffee in a cardboard cup, and asked her if he could get her something before he left, but she said no, giving him a very long hug. Feeling tears, he smiled and left without looking at her. She didn't need to see how sad he was, too, although she probably knew it anyway.

He sat at his work table looking at the collection of photos of four corpses, three decent townspeople and one who was like a son to him. Four murdered in just a few days, and in a town with hardly any history of murders over its one hundred and eighteen years of incorporation. "Holy Mother of God," Al mumbled to himself. He sat staring at the photos for a few minutes more, and then pulled out one of his Dominican black beauties and lit it up. He took a long deep draw and exhaled a thick cloud of smoke over the grisly pictures. He put the back of his left hand up to his lips, the cigar in his right, and stared an intense laser like stare at them that lasted several minutes. At one point his eyes narrowed, and he yelled out, "Holy shit! I knew it!"

In his excitement, Al jumped out of his chair and his cigar fell out of his mouth, dropping a large salt and pepper colored clump of ash on his white shirt, and then falling to the floor. He carefully stomped out the flame and ran to his bookshelf, pulling out that book on wild animals he had very recently been looking at for reasons he wasn't clear about. But now, he was operating on a hunch—a strong one—that Troy and Larry and Beverly and Carl had been clawed to death, not knifed. The deep slices on their bodies were too uniform, spaced apart evenly, like on a paw of a powerful animal, like a bear, or wolf…or a very large cat…a lion, or panther, or cheetah, or leopard…yes…a bear or a predator cat…not a wolf or a pit bull…too small…a big paw with giant claws…slicing through flesh and sometimes reaching bone. Al shuddered, reached for another black beauty, and opened the book.

Chapter 16

Mary, April, Eunice, Jan, Ashley, Marsha, Andy, and Billy

Mary Marie Hardesty McGinnis reached high into her bedroom closet, her left hand grasping for the handle on her old beat up blue suitcase. It was the one she had no occasion to use for so many years because she and Captain Ted never went anywhere anymore. The one she said was all beat up, like her. She yanked it off the top shelf and as it slid out, it landed gently on her head, and she giggled. She was actually in a pretty good mood, having just decided the night before that as soon as Ted went out to find Captain Morgan today, she would quickly pack whatever she could jam in to that old blue suitcase, including her favorite picture of B illy in uniform, and take off to Lord knows where—to freedom—after so many years in captivity to a loveless, abusive marriage. She knew Ted's round trip to Granite State Spirits took about sixteen minutes, so she worked quickly.

The night before, Ted and the Captain had thrown her on the kitchen floor, screaming at her that he knew she was late getting home from Claire and Marty Dobson's house because she was probably giving him a blow job. A s Mary picked herself up off the floor she softly said, "I'm leaving you."

That was the first time she had ever actually said that to Ted, although she had thought it many times.

Ted, slightly taken aback, paused for a moment, and then yelled, "Yeah, that's right, you old whore! Leave! Go ahead! Hah! Go where? You're an old ugly bitch wherever you go!" He paused for a moment as he headed for the bedroom, and added, "You know I'd kill you if you ever tried, anyway."

As Mary pushed hard to close the bulging suitcase, she smiled, telling herself that maybe he'd kill her, but that either way, she'd be free. She ran out the back kitchen door, out across the small leaf-covered yard, and down Elizabeth Street, heading for the bus station. She knew there would be a bus to Portsmouth in just a few minutes that would take her to a Concord Trailways station where she could connect to a bus to New York, where Ted would never travel to find her ("Full of Fags and Hippies," he would say). Then, when she could afford to, she'd go visit Billy in San Diego, and maybe end up living out there.

Just five minutes before, she had been eyeing the kitchen owl clock that told her she only had less than six minutes left before Ted returned. She looked around the kitchen and living room she had lived in for so many years, full of memories, both happy and horrific, but purposely did not look into their nightmare-worthy bedroom. She took a deep breath, fought back tears, and went out the door to a new life. And now, she was at the bus station, buying her ticket to freedom.

Her hands were shaking with excitement, and the agent at the window thought she might be on drugs.

She arrived in Portsmouth in excellent time, but as soon as she stepped off the bus, she hit a wall physically that made her realize how emotionally spent she was. She decided she should have a good dinner, spend a night in a motel, and catch the early bus to New York the next morning She walked for several blocks, came to a small storefront restaurant called Naomi's Chow House, with a small neon sign in the window with multi-colored tubes of light claiming "Real Home-Cooked Food," and entered.

Naomi proved to be a three-hundred fifty pound Polish woman who obviously loved her own home cooking, and who was taking frequent mouthfuls from a plate of food she had on a shelf behind her as she shared waitress duties with Ella and Toni, two almost as large masculine looking women that Mary immediately and correctly perceived as lesbians. She sat on one of the empty counter seats since all three tables were occupied, and smiled warmly at Naomi, saying, "Hi. Could I please have a menu?" If Ted had been with her they would have already been out on the street because of him declaring that no "lesbo dykes" were going to wait on him.

"Things are on the board, hon," Naomi said, in that heavy breathing way obese people talk.

Mary ordered the baked stuffed haddock, baked potato and peas, and hot tea, and then closed her eyes for a few moments, smiling slightly, as she was enjoying a visual image of herself holding her wonderful Billy, hugging him and kissing the side of his neck the way she did when he was little, hugging him and him hugging her back. She ate her meal slowly, relishing each mouthful of the very first meal of her freedom. On her way to a nearby motel, she imagined Ted might by now be all raged out and in a deep Captain Morgan-induced sleep, and by the time she crawled into bed and turned out the lights, she was sure he was.

Mary never heard the car door opening and closing just outside her room. It was three a. m., and she was in a peaceful deep sleep, sitting with Billy, talking and laughing, on a sunny, sandy California beach.

Back in Willard Notch, Ted McGinnis was, as Mary had thought, in a deep, snoring sleep, reeking of spiced rum. This was preceded by a two hour violent rant, during which he nearly destroyed the entire kitchen and dining room, every breakable glass item in both rooms lying shattered on the floor. During the rant he had screamed at the absent Mary with vile language, death wishes, and vows to kill her, to rip her to pieces and cut her heart out and eat it. Captain Morgan's certainly could loosen one's tongue. As he slept on the living room sofa, blood had run out of a glass cut on his left hand, staining the pale yellow fabric a sickly orange, reminiscent of a Halloween Chinese lantern they had when Billy was a kid.

Mary's bleeding was much more plentiful, with one especially large puddle rendering the tough Berber motel rug soggy. Her San Diego beach: gone. Her hopes for her freedom, her love for Billy, were no more.

* * *

Marsha Zanermann and Andy Hauser were sitting out in their back porch, sipping coffee, bundled up to protect them from the frigid New Haven Fall air. They were holding hands one-handedly as they discussed the horrendous news of Willard Notch. Marsha had just gotten off the phone with Wendy, who filled her in on the latest gory details about Mary McGinnis, found that same morning in a Portsmouth motel. "She was a really sweet person as I remember her," Marsha recollected. "Who would want to slaughter her, and Troy Dobson, and Beverly and Carl?" she asked.

Andy responded in typical fashion with, "I dunno," Marsh."

"You know, honey, I think maybe we were very lucky getting out of that sicko town when we did… I grew up there, and it is so damn weird that none of that kind of crap was happening until after we left."

"Yeah, Babe," Andy offered. Marsha just squeezed Andy's hand harder, and stared off into the leafless trees beyond their fence, wondering how Rob was doing with all this. He was a very good kid that she knew felt things very deeply, and Wendy had sounded a little worried about him in their recent phone calls.

"Do you want to go there?" Andy asked.

"No, honey, I just want to sit out here like this, and stop time. Unless one of my kids has a wedding there, I have absolutely no desire to ever set foot again in the Notch."

* * *

"More tea, anyone?" asked April, standing with tea pot in hand, at her dining room table, addressing the three women and one man seated there. Her mother-in-law, Jan Poschner, Ashley Seznicki, and Billy McGinnis declined, all still nursing their first cup. The mood at the table was somber, dialogue limited, and occasional sobs breaking free.

The five of them were all grieving, of course, and also still experiencing that level of shock that allows you basic, adequate functioning, but with a haze of numbness wrapped around each person like an LL Bean winter parka.

"April, do you think we should have Al Fenton here, too?" asked Jan. "He's still the principal investigator as far as I'm concerned, in spite of those Boston FBI guys who have jumped in. And one thing we know about Al is that he really cares."

"I agree," April responded, "but who leads what isn't really up to us. Jan. We have to let the FBI do their thing."

"Do you realize what poor Al had to go through with those know-it-alls in order to establish that we aren't talking about a human killer?"

Those big city smart-asses sneered when he told them his findings, saying the absence of any zoo in this part of the world made it virtually impossible that a big predator cat was roaming the streets of Menard County, New Hampshire. When Al showed the Feds, tape measure in hand, his findings about the pattern of the deep slices on each body, they were impressed, and Al lit up a black beauty victory cigar, the way Red Auerbach used to do with the Boston Celtics. However, because there was little other evidence pointing to a killer cat (no paw prints, no convincing DNA, and definitely no sightings of such an animal anywhere in the State (they did unsuccessfully check out White Mountains mountain cats, but their claws didn't fit the pattern), they still entertained the idea that a human might have engineered the murders to resemble the work of a panther, or jaguar, or cheetah, or leopard... lions and tigers were ruled out for structural reasons. There was no way they could be convinced that an animal could have sought out the victims, especially one way down in Portsmouth, unless controlled and guided by a human. The human they looked at most closely was, of course, Ted McGinnis, a man known to be violent. But after two intense Q and A sessions, they decided he was not a viable suspect.

So who was?

"Right now they have no real suspects," said Billy. "Once they ruled my dad out, they were nowhere."

Billy had flown in from San Diego the day after Mary was murdered, having received a very garbled, drunk, and angry long distance call from his father. Ted stayed drunk through the whole weekend of the brief wake and funeral, and Billy shared no sad or compassionate feelings with anyone in his family, especially his father. Only the people now at the dining room table had comforted him.

Billy continued. "I think we should keep meeting as a group and definitely have Al join us. I think we're the only hope for this town to unravel this nightmare."

"I agree," chimed in Jan... and Eunice... and Ashley... and April.

"Well," said Billy. "I guess we just deputized ourselves."

"Troy would be very happy about this," April declared, and Eunice added, "And very proud of you, April."

April fought back tears, and flashed Eunice an "I love you, too" smile, both women basking in the warm glow of recognition that they both loved and were loved by the same good man, a feeling they were to frequently share.

"You know," said Jan, "every time I pick up Lebowski these days I whisper in his ear, 'Tell me what you know,' and he just looks up at me like I'm crazy. And you know what? I'm not so sure he's wrong."

That feeling resonated with all of them.

The discussion at the table continued a while longer until Eunice said, "Hey you youngsters. You're probably able to do this for hours, but me, I need some sleep."

"I agree," said April. "Let's stop for now, but how about meeting here again tomorrow night after your dinners, like seven or so?"

All agreed on April's plan, and minutes later Eunice and April were standing in the front hall giving each other a silent hug. As soon as the door closed behind Eunice, April felt that dreaded alone feeling, and quickly headed for bed herself.

Chapter 17

Ed and Rob
Marsha and Andy
Sam and Sarah

It was seven-thirty on a chilly Wicker Falls evening, and the three Zanermann's were together in the kitchen, doing after dinner cleaning up, Ed washing, Wendy drying, and Rob clearing off and cleaning the dining room table. No one was talking, until Rob broke the silence by asking Wendy, "Guess who I saw downtown today?"

" Elvis?" she replied.

"Very funny, Wen, very funny."

"Well why not!" she shot back. "There's been a lot of outsiders around this town lately. Law enforcement, media people, curious people traveling through. You don't know who you're likely to run in to."

"Well, it wasn't Elvis. It was Billy McGinnis. Remember him from your elementary school days?"

"Of course I do, and I remember you protected me that day I stepped on his stupid pennant."

"Stupid? The Celtics pennant stupid? I would have been pissed off, too, if you had ruined my C's pennant."

"Oh God, you guys and your silly sports." Rob wondered for a moment just how many times he had heard his little sister ridicule his and their dad's love of sports. The Celtics, Patriots, Red Sox, and Bruins. It didn't matter which was the team of the season, they were all stupid, according to Wendy, and to Marsha, too, when they were kids.

"So why do you think Billy is back in the Notch?" Ed asked.

"How am I supposed to know? I haven't spoken to him in years. Maybe he's here because his mother just got violently murdered by some guy just a few days ago!" she replied sarcastically.

"Some guy?" mocked Rob. "What makes you think it was some guy? Maybe it was some woman. Do you know something the FBI doesn't know?"

"Oh yeah, right! Some woman ripped Larry Boynton and Sheriff Hopkins to pieces, all by her little ol' bitchy self!"

"Wendy! Enough!" yelled Ed. "If you're done drying the dishes, why don't you just go upstairs and read a book, or gab on the phone with your friends."

"Wendy was startled by her father's gruff and nasty tone, and simply said, "Fine!" fighting back tears as she stormed upstairs.

As soon as they heard Wendy's bedroom door close, Ed and Rob almost simultaneously sat down next to each other at the small kitchen table so they could talk softly.

"You okay?" Ed asked.

"Yes, Dad, I'm okay," Rob replied, with a very noticeable edge in his voice.

"Just asking, my boy, just asking."

"Yeah? Well, I've got something I have to ask *you* about, Father, dear. What in god's name happened in your store that night?"

"What did he tell you, Robbie?" Both men were caught short by Ed's use of the name he hadn't called Rob by in at least a dozen years.

"Just that you and he had a long talk, and that while it was sort of edgy at the beginning, by the end of the talk things had smoothed out and you two saw things the same way."

"Yeah, that's about it," Ed replied.

"So what happened to Larry Boynton is my fault? And why Jan's mom and dad? Was that you? And Sheriff Dobson?"

Rob's voice was getting louder as he spoke, his words accelerating.

"STOP!" yelled Ed, and Wendy burst out of her room and yelled down from the stairway, "Will you two please stop? What are you fighting about? Will you two stop with those damned testosterone explosions? Even when Rob was a kid, Dad, you and he would have stupid arguments about sports, and it would scare me and drive Mom crazy. Please!"

"Fine, Wendy, my sweet little girl, go back in your goddamn room and do some knitting, goddamnit! NOW!"

A pang of fear swept through Wendy's being, giving her goosebumps and a cold chilling numbness. Never in her life had her father ever talked to her like that, and her racing thoughts, struggling to be heard over her pounding heartbeats and labored breathing told her something was wrong, very wrong. She went back into her room, closed and locked her door, and started dialing her mother's number. As she did, she could hear that Rob and her dad were still embroiled in whatever they were into.

Marsha's simple "Hello?" allowed Wendy to break into the tears that were jammed up inside her. "Wendy? Baby? What's wrong, honey?"

The call lasted a good twenty minutes, and culminated with Marsha saying, "I'll be there tomorrow. Go to bed, and leave your door locked. I love you, and it will all be okay soon. Good night, Wendy."

Wendy fell asleep fairly quickly, but her dreams were anything but pleasant.

"C'mon, Babe. Going back to that shit hole of a town is a bad idea. You know there's nothing you can do there that will matter."

"Andy, you're asking me to not be there for my daughter, even though she's scared to death up there, and living, possibly, with two crazy violent guys. I have to go."

Andy Hauser knew from Marsha's first response that it was going to be a losing battle to stop her from driving up to the Notch at the crack of dawn. He felt it his duty to at least try, because from everything they were hearing on the news, that place had gone totally haywire, and sounded dangerous.

"Look, honey, I know you're just trying to protect me, but this is Wendy who's in danger. But look, you want to protect me? Let me take your handgun with me. You know I know how to use it, you taught me."

"Oh, Jesus, baby, now you're going there packing a gun? Are you crazy?"

"No, Andy, but I'm afraid Ed is."

"You going to the house?"

"Of course I am, and I'm bringing her back with me."

"She's going to live here with us? Are you kidding, she hates me!"

"She does not hate you. She just sees the breaking up of the family as your fault."

"Oh, because I beat you up and dragged you away from the Notch?"

"C'mon, Andy, let's not do this now. I've got to get some sleep."

Andy softened his tone, told Marsha he was sorry and that he would stop the arguing, and she went to him and whispered in his ear as she hugged him, "Thanks for always being such a good man, Andrew Hauser." They kissed, and Marsha went to bed and would have had a fitful sleep that night, but Handy, Randy Andy Candy, or whatever they called him, eased her into a warm, safe sleep, lying behind her and holding her in that most special spooning position. It was Andy who didn't sleep much this night.

* * *

Sam Kendall was snoring loudly in his recliner, the New England Patriots post-game show still highlighting plays from their big late game come-back victory over the upstart Jacksonville Jaguars, a huge underdog that had the Patriots number through three quarters but couldn't withstand one of those blistering fourth quarters that was the great Tom Brady's trademark.

For Sam to be sleeping at such a time was unheard of in the Kendall household, and Sarah, standing next to his recliner, was worried about him. Besides this sleep thing, he had been acting more irritable and even angry in recent days, and she figured something was going on. Whether it could be his health, or some unspoken situation, she couldn't tell. She did know Doctor Akers was concerned about his blood pressure, and more importantly, she knew that that big-titted slut, Marge Thromeyer, had been his mistress for years. But she never let him know she knew, so why was he getting so irritable with her all of a sudden.

Sam's eyes shot open as he bolted upright in his recliner. "So what the hell do you want now?" he shouted at Sarah.

"Sam, what are you talking about? I don't want anything. I'm just wanting to see if you're alright."

"Alright? Of course I'm alright, what the hell are you talking about? Al ways sneaking around behind my back. Oh Sam, this. Oh Sam, that. Get off my back, bitch!"

Sarah shrunk back from his verbal attack, incredulous that her Sam would ever talk to her like that, and also scared.

Sam got up from the recliner, stormed into their bedroom, and slammed the door hard enough to make several paintings hang crookedly on the living room wall. Something told Sarah, call it instinct or intuition, that she better spend the rest of the night in the recliner, and Sam made sure she did.

* * *

It was just shortly after dawn, and Marsha Zanermann was white-knuckling it on the Mass Turnpike, going at an 80 clip. and keeping an eye on the rear view mirror for cops. Something told her, call it instinct or intuition, that she better get up to the Notch as fast as possible. Just a couple of more hours and she could get her scared little girl out of that shit hole. Andy was certainly right about that.

She decided she would make a quick pit stop at a New Hampshire liquor store and get a few of those little nip bottles… she figured a little liquid courage would be good, and she'd even get one for Wendy, who certainly was no longer just a kid. She struggled to figure out how to deal with Rob… He was still her kid, but she had lost any authority with him, thanks to Ed, who's countless smirking references to "nagging" over the years had their disaffecting influence on Rob.

As she drove on, Marsha got the thought that a man's passive-aggressive behavior, which was Ed's style over the course of their relationship, was every bit as bad as overt male aggression, and it could be equally destructive. She hoped that he at least was still in the passive mode. She would soon find out if he was.

Part IV

MERGER

Chapter 18

Late Fall in Willard Notch, and a Meal at April's

Several days more had passed in the Notch with nothing bad happening. No more murders. No more slicing and dicing. Not much more of anything, as a matter of fact. It was a chance to regroup, as they say, to take some deep breaths of that crisp, clean New Hampshire Fall air.

The FBI was in and out quite a bit, news media also, and Al Fenton, was unofficially serving as interim Sheriff while the Menard County Commissioners were picking Troy Dobson's official replacement. He was spending lots of time on the Internet, soaking up everything he could find on killer cats. At the same time, he was also spending some time on researching State records on crimes in Menard County and the Notch in particular since its days of incorporation. He was also reading the best known memoir of the area back before there were formal written records. His mind was reeling from so much data, so many facts and possible ways of understanding them, but he kept getting back to his original hypothesis, that a killer cat had laid waste to five residents of the Notch, and there was no damn way in hell to explain how that could possibly happen.

Al was trying to get his head together for his dinner time encounter, not with those FBI guys, but rather, with five brave townspeople who wanted to work with him to clean up the Notch from all this horror, and to get at least a taste of revenge, if not a whole meal of it. Fortunately, they were meeting at April's house, and she promised him she'd make a big lasagna. In all her grief, she was still his darlin' April.

When he got to the house, April greeted him at the door, and gave him a welcoming but low energy hug. She was clearly glad to see him, but Troy's murder was robbing her of that wonderful joy and lively energy that was always her trademark. As he hugged her back, he whispered, "How ya' doin, kid," to which she responded with a little extra squeeze but no words, conveying that she appreciated the question but had no easy answer to it. Al got the point.

When he went into the dining room he was immediately greeted by the three women seated there, all of whom got out of their chairs and smilingly extended a hand to him. As he sat himself, Al observed, "Well, I'm just one lucky guy alone here with four lovely women."

All his life he had been a man who visibly, and privately, had been an admirer of women, whether for looks or for skill, always aimed to please, and was free with his words of praise for females. He was always seen as a genuinely good man by all women, and some even noted a touch of feminist thinking in his communications. So, when Ashley, Eunice, and Jan had very muted reactions, feeble smiles, to his words, he was a little taken aback. Sensing this, Eunice told him not to feel embarrassed by that, because, "We women were just sitting here and talking about male chauvinism and how it relates to male misogyny and violence, not a great entry point for a nice guy telling us we're lovely. Hell, Al, I haven't been called lovely since I was six years old."

They all had a good laugh over that, and the April entered the room asking what was so funny, while carrying a platter with a big bowl of salad and a large casserole dish loaded with her perfectly sinful lasagna. Al explained it all to her, and then added, "But I really am the only guy."

"Only for a few minutes," April said. "Billy called to say he was running late but he was on his way. He said he was still trying to clean up the mess in the kitchen from his father's rampage. I feel really bad for him, his mother murdered and his father a walking train wreck."

"Do you guys think he's really comfortable with us?" Ashley asked.

"Why do you ask?" questioned April.

"I'm just not sure. I think maybe he thinks his father did it."

"Or," Al added, "Maybe he thinks my cat theory is absurd. Some people do, you know."

" Well, " Eunice interjected, "I think we do need to come up with a way, Al, to have some underpinnings, some basis to explain why and how."

"Believe me, Eunice, I'm searching for that day and night," Al responded. "I'm even checking out superstitions and myths on Internet, but nothing much comes up, just some stuff about Native Americans believing when there's a lunar eclipse, it's really a jaguar eating the moon. They used to live in North America, but migrated to South America eons ago. They only live there and in Central America now."

Eunice looked absorbed in Al's words for the next several minutes of group banter. Now, April was serving plates of salad and lasagna as she asked Al if he had found anything else on the Internet, and when Al assured her that he hadn't, she said to the group, "Well I have."

All eyes turned to April, but before she could recount her findings, the doorbell rang. "That's got to be Billy. Come on in, Billy, the door is unlocked," she called out. It was indeed Billy, and he came bounding in, greeting everyone, and apologizing for being late. April fixed him a plate of food, and as she passed it to him she said to everyone, "C'mon, let's eat. We'll talk after."

"I vote for that," declared Al. "Best lasagna a man can find!"

The women in the group exchanged quick smiling glances and eye rolling, and then all proceeded to dig in and enjoy the best lasagna a man can find.

* * *

After dinner, which included a unanimously loved peach cobbler that Eunice had brought, and after Ashley and Jan had cleared the table put all dishes in the sink, and after April had brought a large pot of coffee and some cups, spoons, and napkins to the table, she sat and said, "Okay, so here's the stuff I found on the Net."

"First of all, I did research on large cats that kill humans generally, and then I searched out each type thoroughly. Lions, tigers, cheetahs, jaguars, leopards, mountain lions, cougars, pumas. I checked them all, and one breed jumped out at me. Anyone want to guess which one?"

After a pause, Jan offered, "Tigers?"

"Nope!" April answered.

More silence, and then Billy said, "No panthers on your list?"

"Actually, no, Billy. They aren't on my list because I learned that they and the jaguars are the same cat, except for the coloring difference. Jaguars are like golden panthers."

"And panthers are just black jaguars," interrupted Billy. "They are from the same family. Brothers."

"Right," responded April with an amused laugh. But Billy wasn't amused, he had offered his informational tidbit with intentional seriousness, and he went on further.

"I gotta tell you all about a weird dream I had last night, if that's okay. I think it may be really important, and it has me thinking we're dealing with a…, well, you gotta believe in stuff like this to understand about the cat."

"C'mon Billy, get on with the dream," broke in Ashley, who had been having some dreams of her own, only hers weren't weird, they were intense romantic fantasies, all about her and Larry getting married, having four kids, three boys and a girl, being lovers, winning the lottery together, holding each other for hours in silence, in bed. In these dreams the people of the Notch worked through their prejudices and embraced them as the area's first interracial couple, and the four kids were very popular.

"Yeah, well," Billy resumed, "I had a weird dream, and then I started remembering some stuff that really shook me up, and I think it may be important to what we're trying to do. I was taking a nap on my mother's bed when I first got in from San Diego, jet lag, I guess. The bedroom and bathroom were the only rooms my dad didn't trash, although the bathroom was... No, never mind about that." Billy was visibly embarrassed, but continued on. "My parents had twin beds, and even my father's bed was made up and not slept in, so I think he's been too drunk to make it upstairs. or somethin'. So anyway, I was sleeping on my mother's bed, and had this weird dream. It was about my mom. She got attacked and killed by this big killer cat, but she wasn't in that hotel room in Portsmouth. She... she was, um, she was actually at the high school football stadium. It was all empty and dark, and it was raining, and her blood is running out onto the grass and the cat goes running off and is gone and a big bolt of lightning strikes and lights up the field and I can see her face and she's looking right at me and it's like she's wanting me to know something and I think I do and I wake up and then I remember about the Thanksgiving game and I... I..." Billy burst into tears and started shaking, saying only, "My mom...my mom..."

Jan jumped out of chair and grabbed Billy in a tight hug, and she, too, was now crying. and the two continued to cry together, rocking back and forth in that embrace, two grief-stricken babies crying for their lost mommas, and then everyone was crying.

After a few minutes, Billy and Jan sat back down, and April finally broke the silence with a resounding "Well! I think it's time for another round of coffee…Who's interested?"

Al immediately asked if there was any booze she could put in it.

"As a matter of fact I have almost a full bottle of Arrow Coffee Brandy that Troy bought just a few weeks ago. We love that stuff in our coffee on cold snowy nights. And we…"

Now it was April's tears that lent more soul to the proceedings. Eunice got out of her chair and comforted her sobbing daughter-in-law who remained seated.

"I know dear… I know… I know."

The group sat silently for a few minutes, and then Ashley broke the silence with, "Billy, you have more to tell us. Can you do it now, or do we need to stop for tonight?"

Billy responded immediately with, "No, now. I want to do it now."

"Well, we're all with you, Billy. We're all here with you."

"I know, Ashley. It feels like you guys are really my family now."

The room grew silent again for a minute or so, and then, as April splashed Arrow Coffee Brandy ("cheap and delicious," Troy always said) into people's coffee from her dead husband's recently opened bottle, Billy McGinnis resumed his harrowing story.

Chapter 19

Sam and Sarah, and The Men Meet

Sarah Kendall was lying in bed, wearing her floral print silk pajamas, her favorite ones when the weather got cold.

She had seen them in a store window out at the Mall, mentioned how beautiful she thought they were to Sam, who made sure she got them for her birthday on the First of the following month, March. Sam had always felt he was lucky to have married a Pisces because as the books suggested, she was a relatively quiet and internalized woman. You could never be sure at all what her real feelings were about a lot of things, and he benefited from her rarely bitching at him about the kinds of things most women would. If he was late getting home, if he left dirty dishes lying around, and best of all for Sam was that there was no bitching when he hired Marge, even though he knew it really upset her. She would sometimes ask questions, but never complained. It was what he thought of as a "bitchless" marriage, as opposed to a "blissful" marriage, and that was just dandy with him. Sam had been surprised, and eventually furious that Sarah started to act strangely negative toward him right after Larry was murdered, but especially so right after Troy got his. It seemed like she could sense some things, was suspicious of him, and actually had the goddamn nerve to confront him about it. He had flown off the handle and called her a few choice names, screaming at her in a way he never had before and that actually shocked both of them. Since then, it seemed, they were frequently at each other, and Sam found himself mumbling angry and misogynistic things around the house.

But last night, the violent urges he felt inside himself took the cake, alright. She had started in on him about "that Thromeyer slut" that made his blood boil, and here he was now, sitting in the bedroom armchair, looking at his wife lying in bed wearing those beautiful silk pajamas he had bought for her… sliced up like a loaf of white bread, and covered with a thickening claret sauce.

The thought, "Well, at least that bitch is quiet now!" flashed through his mind, then an image of Marge's gorgeous tits, and then a plan on what to do now. He decided not to call that half-assed Sheriff's Department, at least not yet. He pulled out his pocket phone book with numbers for most of his friends and good customers, found the number he was looking for, and made his call.

"Ed, hi. It's Sam Kendall…"

* * *

The men seated at the Kendall dining room table were talking softly, not wanting anyone to hear, and with shades drawn so no one could see them. Sam was seated at the head of the table, where he always sat when it was just him and dear departed Sarah. Ed and Rob Zanermann were seated to his left, and Ted McGinnis to his right. Sam seemed to know that while Ted would be predictably drunk, and maybe smell unpredictably bad, it was essential that he be at their meeting. Sam felt he had a firm grasp on what it was all about with that evil bastard with the black Jaguar, and if he was right, Ted McGinnis was the most important man in Willard Notch.

"So what in hell is going on, Sam?" Ed Zanermann shifted nervously in his seat as he asked that question.

"And why the Christ are we meeting here?" slurred Ted. He had not drawn a sober breath since Mary's death, and that meant a constant flow of Captain Morgan's. Rob cringed as Ted belched loudly after his question. Did he think this was a joke?

"Listen to me, you bastards," growled Sam. "We've all gotten ourselves into a real mess here, with the FBI swarming around town like mosquitoes, goddammit, and that sleaze-ball with the sports car has been playing us like a fiddle, and we need to go underground or something, before the Feds nail us."

"I'm not even sure what that guy did to me, and as for you, Dad, we've talked three times already and I still don't know how he got the whole thing going with you at the beginning." Rob continued, "but the thing he told me that persuaded me the most was that he already knew you and did you a big favor."

All Ed could say was," That sack of shit played me like a fiddle.
"

Ted got out of his chair and addressed the gathering. "Yeah? Hey listen, you jerk-offs, it's really all about the bitches, right? C'mon guys, put the friggin' blame where it belongs! That cat man is one cool guy, right? H e knows what we need and he did all the dirty work, didn't he? We should all be drinkin' a toast to that sleek son-of-a-bitch!"

The dining room fell quiet. The only sound would have been the sound of eyeballs moving around in the men's heads, darting from person to person around the table, each man trying to read the reactions of the other. But eyeballs don't make sounds, and the room stayed deadly quiet for a few minutes more, and then, getting out of his chair, Sam said, "Look, guys. We have to hide the truth here and cover for each other, and we need to have our stories be consistent with each other."

"I agree," Rob declared, "but, I still need to know what the hell happened. What did he do, with my dad, with me, and with you two. I mean I know what happened, but how did he do that, or did he do that, or something else, or what?"

Ted stood up again, albeit on somewhat wobbly legs. "C'mon you guys. We know what he did. I know ezzactly what he did for me, god bless him. He could read my goddamn mind, knew I wanted that bitch dead, and he got it to happen. What else do we need to know, eh?"

"Yeah, Ed responded, "but what's with the killer cat thing, can anyone explain that to me?"

Sam stayed sitting in his chair at the head of the table, and said in a quieter, somber voice, "I think I know."

All six eyes at the table were now fixed on Sam. Sam Kendall, co-owner of Kendall Motors with his wife, Sarah Kendall, open six days a week, and home of the best deals in new and used cars and trucks in the Granite State.

Chapter 20

Billy and the Group

Billy cleared his throat a few times, and then resumed his story.

"After that dream, it set me to thinking about my mom and something that happened at the Jaguars Thanksgiving Day game a bunch of years ago, but I suddenly remembered it all, clear as a bell. I could even see it, and feel it."

He continued, "Right after I had the dream in her bed I said to myself, what a weird dream. I mean like a dream about my mom on a football field? Like, I mean, she always seemed to hate football. Not basketball, or track, or baseball, just football."

"Billy, do you think your mother simply worried that you might get hurt if you played football? You know you guys get pretty violent in a sport like that." Eunice was trying to use a little motherly wisdom to help him figure things out, but Billy immediately addressed Eunice.

"No, you don't understand, Ms. Dobson."

"Please just call me Eunice."

"Okay, Eunice, but you just don't understand. My mom wasn't afraid for me with football. I can tell you for sure, she was afraid for herself."

"How can you be sure?" Al asked.

"If you were there that Thanksgiving and saw how she was trying to get me to not go with my dad to the game but to stay back with her, you'd be sure, too. I mean she was just about shaking, and when I tried to get her to come with us, she pulled way back and looked at me with that 'deer in the headlights' look, you know? I mean it was really crazy that she wouldn't come. She came to a few of my basketball games with my dad, and seemed to enjoy herself, and she was always happy if we ever did anything as a family, because it didn't happen very often at all. She always tried to get my dad to take me places, but on this day, when my dad told her to stay home, that he would take me to the game, she wasn't happy at all, and was really, really upset."

Billy paused for a sip of that delicious warm spiked coffee, and continued. That night she and I talked for a little while, and she seemed very sad as she started to explain her behavior earlier that day. I don't think she ever got to finish what she was wanting me to know, because at some point my dad came into the room, overheard a little of what she was telling me, and started yelling at her, 'Oh no, you stupid twat, you're not telling him that same old bullshit story about your mother are you?' My mom looked like someone had just stabbed her in the heart, she stopped talking, gave me a hug and said, 'It's okay Billy,' kissed the top of my head, and went upstairs to their bedroom and closed the door. My dad just said, 'Dumb-ass woman!' and went into the kitchen to refill his Captain and Coke, and turned on the TV. My mom and I never talked about it again."

Billy paused for a moment, his eyes filled with tears. April asked him if he felt okay telling them whatever his mother did get to tell him, and he nodded yes, and continued.

"She said that she was really sorry about how she had behaved, and said she hoped she hadn't scared or upset me, and I lied and told her no, that I was fine. I wish now that I was old enough back then to tell her that I was very upset and we needed to talk more, but I was too young to realize what she was trying to talk about, but I do now. I sure as hell do. The part she did get to tell me was that she really couldn't go to the football game because when she was entering high school, her mother told her that something very bad had happened to her when she was in high school, and that's why she just couldn't go and watch the Jags play. When she herself was a cheerleader, my grandmother never came to see her perform at football games."

Billy paused again to take a deep breath and also wipe a few tears off his cheek. His countenance changed as he continued, shifting from sad to angry. "Oh, I think I forgot to mention something important in my dream. Lying there dead in the rain on the stadium grass, her cheerleader's skirt was up near her neck."

"Oh my god," said Jan.

"Oh Billy, I am so sorry," said Eunice.

"Goddamnit!" said Al.

April and Ashley didn't say anything, but their faces registered shock.

"So do you guys see what I'm saying? My dream somehow was my mom finishing her story. My grandma was raped by Jaguar football players, and my mom gets murdered by a killer cat. No, not a panther or a tiger or a lion, a jaguar, a jaguar killed her, I know it, I just know it!"

Once again, the room fell silent. It was broken a few minutes later when Al, interim Sheriff of Menard County, said, "Well I'll be goddamned!"

At that point April suggested they break for the night, and everyone feeling emotionally spent, agreed. They also agreed to meet again the next afternoon, same place. As people left, each one stopped to give Billy a hug, and to tell him they appreciated his bravery. Al added that yes, his dream was very, very important. April added that she wished she could take his pain away, but knew she couldn't, and confessed to him that she was planning to have more Arrow Coffee Brandy later that night. Billy replied with a slight smile, "Just don't do that Captain Morgan's shit. It's poison."

Chapter 21

Marsha and Wendy

Marsha took a sip of her coffee and broke a small piece off the Texas toast with strawberry jam that she was slowly eating as she and Wendy continued to review the events of the day before in order to make sense of it all. Wendy was likewise eating breakfast slowly, in fact just toying with her scrambled eggs and bacon. Her appetite was just not there, even for her beloved bacon... still reeling emotionally from yesterday's horror show. They were having breakfast at the small coffee shop connected to the Scenic View Motel, about fifteen miles outside Willard Notch.

They had decided to stay there only after Wendy talked her mother into it. Marsha had wanted to head straight back home immediately after leaving "The Wicker Falls Crazy House," as she called it, but Wendy refused to do that, unwilling to abandon the only town and only home she had ever known.

"We can't just leave, Mom, What about Rob? I know you hate Dad, but you know there's something wrong with Rob, and we need to be here so we can help him."

Marsha argued that it looked like a hopeless and also dangerous situation to her, and that being safely in her home with Andy would be the best thing for them to do. Wendy, expressing no great love for Randy Andy and with lots of begging, got her mother to reluctantly relent.

"So, my dear daughter, here we are, still in New Hampshire. So what do you think we should be doing right now that may help something, someone, anything?"

"I don't know, Mom, but there's got to be something."

"Well, if I had a gun I could think of a thing or two."

"Mom! Stop it!" Wendy exhorted Marsha.

"Alright, Wendy. Look, I'll go up front to pay our bill and then let's go to the Sheriff's Department or to one of those cute FBI guys and tell whoever about the absolutely wonderful evening we had at the house yesterday. Why, I thought we might both die in that house last night, the only home you've ever known!"

"Alright, let's do that. But Mom, what are we going to do about Lebowski? We need to get him out of there."

"It would be nice dear, but frankly, I think he's closer now to your father and your brother than he ever was before, and at one point he looked like he was going to attack me, his mother, who took great care of him when he was younger. It's like all that loving never happened."

"Mom, I know Lebo was pretty strange last night, but look who he's been with lately, it's a wonder he's still breathing."

"Look Wendy, let's go," Marsha said as she walked over to the area near the entrance with the cash register.

As they were getting into Marsha's car in the Motel parking lot, Wendy blurted out, "Mom, did my dad ever have an affair with Beverly Poschner?"

"What? Why are you asking me that?" Marsha looked dumbfounded as she wondered why Wendy would ever think such a thing.

"Mom, can we please stop the cover-up here. You expect me to believe that Dad never cheated on you?"

Marsha paused, and replied, "I didn't say that he never cheated. I asked why ask about Beverly, of all people."

"Mom, because Beverly and Carl Poschner got all sliced up, and I'm trying to understand why!" She continued on. "I'm sure my lovely brother had something to do with the Larry Boynton slice-up because he had a very clear motive. From things I've overheard at my 'home sweet home,' I'm pretty sure Dad was responsible for the Poschner massacre, but I can't figure out why. I thought maybe you'd know. My God, Mom, I've been living with murderers!"

"Well actually, I had heard that after Andy and I left, your dad developed a thing for Beverly, and that he had tried hitting on her a bunch of times, but she was never interested. One person had said he heard your dad go into a rage in the shop after he hung up on a phone call with her. Your dad didn't hear the guy come in, and I guess he thought he was alone, and screamed 'you're a goddamn bitch, Beverly' at the phone. Maybe it was another Beverly, but knowing your father, I doubt it."

"What now, Mom?"

"Well, honey, I think we should pay Jan Poschner a visit."

"No. No, I don't want to see her. She's probably to blame for this whole mess."

"How do you mean?" Marsha listened intently as Wendy ran through the sequence of events that began with her eavesdropping on the conversation between Jan and Ashley, and her belief that it culminated, she now was convinced, in the brutal slaying of Larry Boynton.

"Oh my god, Wendy, why didn't you tell me about this before?"

"I don't know, maybe something in me that didn't want to be the one to tell you your first-born child is a killer? Or that in a way I put him up to it?"

"Stop it! Stop this bullshit, Wendy. You're to blame for NONE of this, and I know your brother is not a murderer. And while I can't honestly say I am as sure about your father, I have never thought of him as a murderer, ever!"

Wendy fell into her mother's arms, now sobbing. "I don't know what to believe any more."

"I know... I know..." soothed her equally confused mother. "C'mon, let's go." she said.

"Where?"

"To see Al Fenton. He's the closest thing to a Sheriff you have now in this shithole."

"MOM!"

"I'm sorry, Wendy, let's go."

Marsha was surprised how easily that pejorative had roiled off her tongue. God knows she had heard it enough times from Andy who never had a good thing to say about Willard Notch. When she would remind him that the Notch was where he found her, her whom he referred to as the 'jewel of my life," he would simply say yes, but that was the shithole from which he had to rescue her. At this point, she would definitely have to agree.

Later that morning Al urged them to be at April Dobson's for the next meeting later that day, and Marsha ended up agreeing.

"Thanks, Mom," Wendy said to Marsha.

Marsha responded with, "God alone knows whatever it is that we're getting into."

Al added, "And God alone will be our guide."

Chapter 22

Eunice's Plan

April began the gathering, by saying Grace over the gigantic tureen of steaming fish chowder and ladling out bowls for everyone. At the same time, she welcomed their two newcomers, Marsha and Wendy. It was clear from the start that there was a level of discomfort in everyone at the table, all eight, six women and two men, five mourners and three, and three what? One a cop and two... two who?

Everyone had somehow worked their way into the identical thought process that left six people confused, Only Al and Marsha understood the issue, and Al decided to grab for the elephant in the room.

"Well," he began, "You're all probably wondering why I brought these two ladies to our powwow tonight, so let me explain."

Eunice's head snapped back a little when Al mentioned powwow, her eyes slightly narrowing and brow furrowing for a moment or two, and then whatever the thought was, it passed through, and she re-focused on Al's continuing words.

"I know Marsha and Wendy aren't in the same boat as you other guys, because they haven't had somebody they really cared about get murdered. But they're here because, like everyone else living in the Notch, they are connected to this weird nightmare we're living through. Why even Marsha here, who lives hundreds of miles away, has an important story to tell, and we damn well better listen to her when she tells us."

"Yeah, well I know she's Rob Zanermann's mother, and I'm sure as hell that he's one of our murderers!" declared Ashley emphatically, with Larry Boynton firmly in her mind.

"Whoa, Ash," Jan interjected. "Go slow. I think Ed Zanermann has his hands dirty, too, but remember everything we know from you, Al, says that the murders were committed by a killer cat, not a human."

"That' right," Al responded to Jan.

"Okay, Jan, you're right. Sorry, everyone.," Ashley conceded.

"So, they aren't the murderers, but they sure as shit are key perpetrators or delivery boys, or something for the horrible violence that has cursed our city."

"It certainly does feel like a curse, doesn't it?" added Eunice, her eyes once again revealing how deep in thought she was.

"Listen! Please listen," Wendy exhorted the group. "We know my father and brother were involved in this, and Billy, your father is, and maybe Mister Thromeyer or Sam Kendall or both of them. We know there's something really weird going on with some of the men in this town, and nobody is safe!"

"Please, everyone ," Marsha broke in. " Like Al said, Wendy and I have some stuff we can tell you about just how absolutely angry and crazy Ed and Rob have become, and dangerous, too, we think."

"Listen everyone, I think we already know how bad things are, but we don't have the vaguest idea how to deal with it."

It was April, standing up at the table, trying to get some semblance of order back to the meeting. "I think before anything else happens, Marsha and Wendy need to hear Billy's story."

All agreed, and Billy once again brought the group to silence as he finished. Wendy's "Oh my God!" eventually shattered the dark quiet of the speechless group after a few minutes.

"So what do we do?" asked Marsha.

"I don't think any of us has the vaguest idea," Ashley offered.

More silence followed, until a quiet voice calmly stated, "I do."

All eyes turned to Eunice Dobson, the oldest member of the group, and now, apparently, the boldest, too.

"April, honey, that chowdah was really great, don't ya know," she said in her best Downeast Maine accent that always got people chuckling. Even now, in this deadly serious group she got a few, and she added, "Thank you, Lord. We all need to lighten up a little before we head off to showdown hill."

"Showdown Hill?" Al asked.

"Well, yeah," Eunice responded, " you can call it any damn thing you want, but what I'm talking about is wherever that point of no return is once we get moving with this."

Even Eunice herself was caught off guard by the edge in her words. She quickly realized, just one quick step ahead of the others that she was doing what often got called "rising to the occasion," or "stepping into the role," in this case, the leadership role. Her voice was strong and self assured, and she knew she was now the one who would save Willard Notch if anyone could.

"April, dear, would you please make a big pot of coffee, and how about our adjourning to the living room?"

"That's fine with me, Mom."

April's mouth hung open for a moment, stunned by having just called her mother-in-law "Mom" for the first time ever. Feeling no need to discuss the obvious in this very personal moment, they both just smiled, briefly clasped hands, and then moved with the others into the living room. Within a few minutes they all had either a mug of coffee or a glass of Moxie, Northern New England's native cold soda, sitting in a variety of seats more comfortable than the hard-back dining room chairs.

"Okay everyone, I'm just going to talk for a while and try to lay it all out for you, the way I see things. So just let me talk with no questions or comments until I'm done, and then we can kick it all around and decide if it really will be our plan, Okay?"

Seeing a unanimous okay in the group, she continued.

"I've been thinking about this non-stop since our first get-together. I simply cannot stop thinking about it, and I suspect that's true for the rest of you."All heads nodded agreement. "But ever since Billy, here, told us about his dream and Mary's story about her mother, I've been thinking about it in a whole new way. To cut to the chase, I think we're dealing with something more than an animal from a zoo escaped and on the loose. I think we all know that, right Al?"

"We do, Eunice, we do."

"And the FBI knows it too, Al?"

"I don't know what they're thinking these days, Eunice." Al shrugged, and continued. "Lately they're acting like it's slowly but surely becoming a cold case. I mean they still see it as a hot case with immediate serial threat, what with the curfews, and call-a-neighbor stuff and extra law enforcement surveillance in place, but they're beginning to bog down with the killings, having stopped cold since Billy's mom, and not a single lead to follow right now. So they're here, that's for damn sure, but as for right now, that's about the only thing that's sure."

"Okay, so we're dealing with something where's there's no concrete, just a lot of mud, right Al ?" Getting a big nod of agreement from Al, Eunice resumed her attempt to develop a plan. "For me, there's a lot of pieces here that add up to suggest we aren't dealing with just real physical world stuff, but rather some real supernatural stuff, some other worldly stuff, spiritual issues or forces at work, and we've got to deal with it at that level." The group reaction was instant, a cacophony of noise, the chatter of seven people struck by Eunice's words, pushed into a state of emotionality, and if not frenzy, pretty close to it. Eunice waited it out, telling herself this was what she hoped for, that it was striking home for them in some way. If they had thought they were just listening to the cockamamie ideas of an old lady, they would have laughed, or made some snide remarks, or just been uncomfortably quiet. But here, they were, jabbering away, in a hubbub of confusion in an attempt to make sense out of what they had just heard. When it started to die down, she continued.

"I know some of you must be thinking poor Eunice, she's really lost her mind. But I need to tell you guys know I haven't. I believe I have found it, not lost it. I have found that part of my mind that is more soul, heart, and intuition, than logical. I don't know what to call it, but I believe in it, and when I found it, I knew I had to say something at the risk of being laughed at. And then when a couple of you used certain words tonight, I took them as a sign that I didn't just need to say something. I needed to DO something, and that's what I'm doing right now, trying my damnedest to take over this meeting and tell you what we all need to do to fix this Willard Notch horror."

Eunice paused for a moment to sip her coffee, not to help her stay awake, because right now she correctly believed she was very wide awake and could stay that way for many many hours.

She needed that sip because her mouth had become dry from that hyper-aroused state that some call an adrenalin rush that can dry out the mouth of anyone, from a ballet dancer, to a kid in a spelling bee, to a soldier in combat, or to a heavyweight boxing champion, dry as an old boot.

Then she continued.

"Now those of you who know me know how much I love to read. And those of you who know me really well, like you, April, you tell 'em, my favorite writer by far is Stephen King." April nodded agreement. "Now besides him being a neighbor up in Maine, and him being a life-long Democrat, just as I am, I also love his writing, especially in his stories that involve mystical stuff, supernatural stuff, like curses, which someone mentioned tonight, He's written about them and there's other writers and movies that really get into it. Just one that comes to mind is one he wrote about the desecration of Native American burial grounds, and the curse that followed. I think that one flashed into my mind, Al, when you used the word powwow before."

"You've got my attention, Eunice," Al broke in. "I've wondered about that myself."

"Thanks, Al. You represent law enforcement here, and I welcome your support. So, I'm a Democrat and I believe in a democracy, including right here. So I want to get you guys to participate in this. Anybody here have any ideas about what type of curse we might be dealing with in the Notch?"

The ensuing silence lasted for only a few moments before Ashley jumped in. "Well, I would be convinced of racism with how Larry got murdered, nothing new in our Nation's history, but everyone else murdered was white, so I guess I'm not sure."

"Who else?" asked Eunice.

Another moment of silence, and then, "I think I know, for sure." It was Billy. "It's my grandmother, isn't it Eunice?"

"Yes, Billy, I believe it is," replied Eunice in a slightly hushed voice.

"Okay," said Jan, " but why do you think it's that? And what do my parents have to do with Billy's grandmother ?"

"It's a little complicated, Jan honey, so bear with me while I explain more. Let me first lay out for you right now, that the killer cat is no panther. As I've said, we're dealing with a jaguar, but not a solid, material jaguar, but a spiritual one driven by evil forces that enable it to actually kill people. Why am I so sure it's a jaguar? Because Mary McGinnis 's mother had been raped in high school many years ago by Jaguars, our very own football heroes, with their satin jackets with a growling jaguar on the back. Oh yeah, and "GO JAGS" on the front. Now you all know my own dear son, Troy, also a victim of the violence here, proudly wore that jacket and was a big school hero, but I see no reason to believe that simply wearing that jacket makes a man a perpetrator of violence against women. As far as I know, Troy was a very kind and gentle man. Am I right, April honey?"

April nodded and said, "Absolutely."

There was lots of murmuring in the group for a few minutes, and then Eunice resumed.

"So what kinds of thoughts are you folks having right now?"

Marsha was the first to speak.

"Okay, so it must be a jaguar, but why is it killing the people it is instead of the players who raped Sue Hardesty ?"

"Because if it did that, it would mean that the jaguar is a revenge force, and I don't think it is. I think it's a force that is actually perpetuating the evil violence that caused Sue Hardesty's rape. The revenge part, Marsha? I think that has to be where we come in."

The group murmured again.

"Okay. I'll buy that," Marsha responded, "but how come there was nothing like that in the Notch for so many years after that rape until just a few weeks ago? What reactivated it?"

"That's exactly the right question, Marsha, and I believe I know the answer, but my own personal belief system comes into play here."

"Go for it!" urged Marsha. "I'm listening."

"Okay, so, Wendy, honey, I hope you can listen to this without freaking out, although from things you and your mom were describing to us earlier, you might not be shocked to hear this. I believe that the evil involved in the rape never left the Notch, but it's been around at a low level, like in your dad, Billy, until YOUR dad, Wendy, triggered it with his rage. I am sure, from the bits and pieces the FBI picked up, somebody in town told an FBI guy, who was asking around about this creepy guy in a black Jaguar sports car that some people have seen around town and were suspicious of, was first spotted one night parked outside your dad's shop he reached out on that cursed internet for a hit man, of all things, who actually came here in that black Jaguar car, of all things, and conjured up enough male anti-female rage for the whole of Menard County, for god's sake. Marsha, I would think it would have been you he wanted dead, and you know why, but instead of that, it crossed over to Beverly Poschner. I won't try to guess why."

"But why my dad?" interrupted Jan.

"I think he got killed only because he was there, Jan. I think the goal was your mom."

"But why her?" a puzzled Marsha asked.

"Because, Marsha," Eunice continued, "the whole town knew he developed a wicked desire for her after you skipped town with that Hauer kid."

"He's not a kid, Eunice."

"No matter, Honey, Ed must have been rejected or something by Beverly and that's why his rage killed her."

Ashley chimed in with, "And Rob Zanermann's rage had to be what killed Larry." She said no more, as Jan, sitting next to her kicked her ankle.

"Yes, Ashley, but let's leave it at that, at least for now, Eunice replied." Jan, needing to change the topic, asked Eunice, "So why Sheriff Dobson, your boy, April, your husband? Was he getting too close to the truth?"

"I don't think that was it."

"No," Al cut in. " He and I were not even close to figuring out what happened to Carl and Beverly and Larry. When he got killed he had just finished up interviewing Sam Kendall and Marge Thromeyer out at the car place, just to see if he could get some sort of lead, and he had come up empty, he told me."

"So why our Troy?" April asked the aging women standing before the group as its new harbinger of truth.

"April, darlin', we lost our Troy, I believe, because of Sam Kendall's jealous rage. We know Sam has had a thing with Marge for many years, poor Sarah, and we also know Marge had strong hankerings for Troy."

"Damned right she did!" April tossed in.

"So it's not that big a stretch to assume that Troy's visit out there triggered Sam. What actually happened I don't know, and April, I hope we agree we really don't need to get into that with Marge Thromeyer."

April gave a gentle nod.

"And so Billy, it goes without saying that your dad's venomous rage had to be what brought your mom down."

"Agreed," Billy said quietly, his head nodding, his eyes narrowing, and his teeth clenched.

Again, a silence fell over the group, until Billy asked what Eunice knew the group had to do. He specifically had used the word "knew" rather than "thought", he explained, because everything in him told him that Eunice really knew what they had to do to stop the killings, and avenge his grandmother's rape. When Eunice went on to explain why seeking revenge for Mary's rape was definitely the key next step, no one in the group was surprised, and no one in the group questioned it.

* * *

As the group slowly filed out of April's house on a bitter cold seven-eighths moonlit night, they all repeated back to Eunice the agreed upon plan, to convene at eight p. m. the next night at Jaguar Field, wearing warm but removable jackets, and bringing matches, a small pad of sticky-notes, a pen, and a small metal bowl.

Eunice herself agreed to bring a tent, and April, some fire wood.

These details had all been worked out under Eunice's guidance and with the use of April's small green chalk board she and Troy used to use to leave messages for each other. There was hugging, but no smiling or laughing. The group was deadly serious, as it would need to be.

April gave the new group leader a big hug and told Eunice how proud she was to be her daughter-in-law. Eunice simply responded with a "Thanks, hon," but as she approached her car in the driveway, she turned and said, "April, honey, you ain't seen nothin' yet!"

Chapter 23

The Strategy of the Clawless

"So what are we going to do with them goddamn bitches, and the stupid fat man cop?" asked Ted McGinnis.

"Shut up and sit down, Ted. That's what we're trying to figure out." It was Ed Zanermann admonishing the rum-soaked, foul-smelling grieving widower, "Testosterone Teddy," as the others in the small group had dubbed him, which he loved. It was an honor, he felt, to be seen as the man, the real man in the group with the biggest supply of that miracle hormone that can make a man screw all day and beat up all night on any woman you put in front of him... or start a war... or piss on a hooker... or knife a colored guy, or whatever.

Ed was seated at his kitchen table with Rob, Sam, and Testosterone Teddy. These four horseless apocalyptic men had agreed they have to develop a defensive action plan as soon as possible, because it was sort of in the Fall Notch air that people would probably be coming after them soon real soon.

"So listen," Ed began, "I've done everything I can to get in touch with Jagman to have him come back here to help us, but nothing on the internet brings him up, and unless he just sort of pops in like he did that night in my shop, I think we're on our own."

"Listen Ed," said Sam, "there's no physical evidence that we did anything to those people, and if you guys can just help me dispose of Sarah, I think we're all okay. Why no one even knows she's dead."

"Yeah," added Ted, "just tell people the old twat went on a long vacation." He chuckled as he talked.

"Shut the Christ up, you goddamned rummy!" Sam retorted.

"Dad, I think Sam is right. I mean even we ourselves aren't really sure about how it all went down, so who in the world can prove us guilty of anything?"

After a few moments of thought, Ed agreed with his son, as did the other two men.

In no way could criminal intent be confused with a crime. No way!

So, their defensive plan was all set: get rid of Sarah, and then just go about their business as usual.

"Shit," said Ted in support of the plan. "That's what I've been doin' for years, ramrod my old lady, or beat the crap out of her, and the next day just be normal, like nothing ever happened. It's really easy."

Ted paused, realizing that there was a slight twitch of sadness he felt around the idea that he wouldn't have old Mary around to use anymore.

"Aw, fuck it all. Where'd I put my bottle of Captain?" The others exchanged quick glances with each other, a little uncomfortable with how far gone Testosterone Teddy was.

"Okay. So do we need to develop a shared story?" Ed asked. "Or is it every man for himself?"

A shared story would take forever," Sam observed. "Let's just sit tight after dumping Sarah, and hope for the best."

The four agreed, and as they were leaving the Zanermann home to head for the Kendalls', Sam added, "It's nice that we men can stick together."

That night, a strange, handsome intense man driving a black Dodge Viper was approaching Bucky's Liquors, a small package store in Baton Rouge, Louisiana. Bucky Faison, the owner, was inside, bagging a bottle of Captain Morgan's Spiced Rum for a customer, but thinking about what he could do with his mother's life insurance money, if only that old bitch... The customer, Arnold Madore, left the store, clutching his precious cargo, and muttering to himself that if that dumb baby factory started bitching at him again about his drinking too much, he would swat her with the Captain's vessel and leave her and those four whining brats forever, and head to New Orleans with that ultra hot Bessie Desjardins kid. He was unaware of the black vehicle that was just pulling into the parking lot as he started his five minute walk home.

Chapter 24

The Night of Reckoning

The light drizzle of rain gave everything a shiny exterior in the full moonlight, and while it was "New Hampshire cold," as people in central and northern New Hampshire called it, it was still above freezing, making the grounds at the football field soggy, but not slippery. It was also somewhat windy, but not overwhelmingly so, maybe twenty miles per hour.

Eunice Dobson sat in her dark green Chevy pick-up with the motor running so as to keep enough heat coming to fight the damp chill of the evening.

She was waiting for the other seven people to show up for what Eunice knew would be a night to remember. She was wearing a fleece lined nylon winter jacket she bought at LL Bean's a dozen years ago, and damned if it didn't still look like brand new. She always told herself Bean's had a lifetime replacement offer on things they made because they were confident you would never need to replace it. Martin had the same pair of Bean boots he got when he was in high school, and Troy... Her mind stalled with the thought about her handsome baby. First were a few tears, but then came a tightening of her jaw and a gritting of her teeth, and the satisfying thought that yes indeed, this would definitely be a night to remember.

In the back of the pick-up she had a few pieces of birch firewood, which she always thought smelled the best, burned the best, and was closest to her heart. To whatever extent she had Native American blood pumping through her veins (quite a few Northern New Englanders correctly laid claim to that), the birches felt spiritually meaningful, as did certain animals and birds, and some things she grew in her garden. She planned to add the birch to the firewood April would be bringing. She also had a box of long wooden fireplace matches, some rope, a well-sharpened hatchet, and a beige vinyl tent that would certainly be plenty large for the evening's purposes. The group numbered eight members, a size she had heard many experts on how groups work best say was ideal for small group success. She thought to herself about how wonderful that will be if they 're right.

The first car pulled in to the lot. It was Al.

"Evening Eunice. I guess we old -timers are more anxious to get started than the young'uns."

"Yesiree Bob," Eunice replied, keeping Al's tongue in cheek country lingo going. A moment later, Marsha and Wendy were the next to pull in to the lot.

Marsha rolled down her window and said, "Evening, folks. Is this the place where Willard Notch is getting its clock cleaned tonight?"

Eunice replied, "Honey, you better believe it!"

"Hi, you guys," Wendy called out from the passenger side.

"Glad you're here, Wendy," Al responded.

April was the next to arrive, with a healthy load of firewood and a hug for her two favorite elders.

As April and Al were getting the tent off Eunice's truck, Jan and Ashley pulled in, greeted everyone, and were soon helping pitch the tent. Now, only Billy was missing.

"So now, where is that young man?" Eunice wondered out loud.

"Oh I'm sure he'll be right along," Jan said, but Ashley added, "I just hope his crazy old man hasn't done anything to him."

"Billy's crazy old man is done doing anything to anyone, if I have anything to do with it, and I definitely do. We all do!"

All eyes turned toward Eunice, and after a brief moment, April yelled out, "Tonight's the night!" and soon eight people were yelling in unison that this night was the night indeed. Fourteen hands were warmed by vigorous applauding, and seven voices were soon a little raspy from cheering.

Soon the tent was finished, and everyone pitched in bringing pieces of firewood inside the tent, piling it up in the middle.

Just as Eunice was placing her pieces of birch on the top of the pile, Billy pulled up. "Thank god he's here," murmured Eunice.

Everyone greeted him with hugs just outside the tent "Sorry I'm late," he told the group, "but I had to wait until my dad went out to the liquor store so I could get something I really needed to bring here."

"What is it, Billy?', asked Wendy."It's not that old Celtics pennant that I ruined, is it?"

"Oh my god, you do remember that?"

"Of course I do, and in case I never said it to you, I really am sorry…now."

After a few moments of good natured laughter, Billy's countenance became very serious, and he told everyone he had to get something from his car.

When he returned, he was carrying a jacket, a standard high school football jacket. A Jaguars jacket.

"This was mine when I was in high school, then my dad grabbed it for himself when I went into the Navy. He's considered it his ever since. My mom had tried to get it back to me for years, usually at Christmas time, but as far as he was concerned, it was his. And so I had to steal it out of his closet to bring it here." Billy handed it to Eunice with outstretched arms, saying, "Eunice, I believe you know what this is for."

"Billy, my boy, you know I do, and it will help our soul-inspired plan enormously."

Eunice's referring to the plan as "our" was evidence that this newly empowered woman leader had maintained a sense of humbleness not often associated with male leaders, who as Wendy's Bubbie Zanermann used to say, were very "ego*testicle*."

Carrying Billy's jacket in her arms like it was the sacrificial offering it was meant to be, Eunice led the eight tribesmen into the tent. After the other seven had seated themselves in the lotus position (a bit of a struggle for Al) in a circle around the large stack of firewood, she draped the jacket over the top of the pile and startled everyone, except Billy, when she yelled out, "We're here, Sue, we're here!"

Her goal of setting the tone for the night seemed to have worked well, she thought, as she seated herself, completing the circle. Starting with the person to her right, which was Jan, she asked each person to stand, light a long wooden match, and toss it into the woodpile. Soon the woodpile, replete with eight thin splinters of wood, was ablaze, and generating enough heat for everyone to get down to shirts and blouses, a pile of their jackets and sweaters now off to the side. As the Jaguar jacket ignited fully, Eunice instructed the group to stand in the circle holding hands and allow some silent time for reflective thought. As the group stood in silence, beginning to sweat from the fire's growing heat, Eunice remembered some Native American man from way back in her past, who exactly she couldn't recall, who said that more truth happens in one sweat lodge than in one hundred Congressional hearings. It probably was around the time of the Army/McCarthy hearings or maybe Watergate. After several more minutes of silence, Eunice simply said to the group, "Repeat after me!

"*Oh Lord of Darkness and Evil, With the Stealth of a Giant Killer Cat, Meet Thy Fate! The Fate You Will Forever Meet When People of Love and Good Faith Rise Up Against You! In the Names of Bev-*

erly Poschner, Carl Poschner, Larry Boynton, Troy Dobson, Susan Hardesty, and Mary Hardesty McGinnis. We the Faithful Banish You Forever from Willard Notch, Wicker Falls, and Wherever Else You Abide in the Dark Corners of the Human Soul."

What followed was several minutes of a very deep and sober silence. Then this circle of the faithful finished on a note of positive energy. When Eunice conclude with, "So, folks, we're going to cross that goal line, and the Jaguars of the universe will be defeated." Eunice figured this group, including herself, was not accustomed to reciting curses in a circle around a sweat lodge type fire, and might need a little energizing to be able to move on into the other part of her plan for the night. When everyone cheered as Al yelled, "Touchdown for the good guys!" she knew she succeeded.

"Alright, everyone, let's get this tent down and put away without hitting our fire. We don't want to burn the tent, and we still need the fire. You'll probably all have to help out to accomplish that."

Everyone did, after donning their outer wear, and soon they were a circle of eight standing outside around a small bonfire. Smoke was billowing up into the bitterly cold night air, with an intermittent ring made up of the visible steam from human breathing. The wind was more brisk now than when they started, and somehow it added to the already pronounced mystical quality of these proceedings on the five yard line of a high school football field.

* * *

Eunice next instructed everyone to go to their vehicles, and using their pens and notepads, write on as many pieces of paper as they wanted, the names of people they wished to excoriate (one of Eunice's favorite words from crossword puzzles that she had to define for some in the group), and write as much about them as they wanted, and then return to the circle with their papers and the small bowl she had told them to bring. It was a full ten minutes before the group had reassembled around the fire, bowls and papers in hand. Clearly, they all had taken the task seriously. April then distributed a long wooden match to each person.

"When I call your name step forward up to the fire, and place your bowl on the ground in front of you. Read whatever you have written on each piece of paper and then place each piece in your bowl. Then place one of these small stones from this field, which I gathered tonight, on top of the papers to hold them in place against the wind. Later, we will summon that wind to help us." One by one, as she called their name loudly and clearly, each person did as she asked.

"Billy McGinnis."

"Theodore McGinnis. Damn you for abusing and torturing my mother for years!" And then, "Death to you, you evil cat, for doing my father's bidding, and a damning curse on all the football Jaguars who raped my grandmother, Susan Hardesty. Dear Lord above, blitz those pigskin pigs for the rest of their days."

"Jan Poschner."

"Ed Zanermann, damn you for having my parents murdered because you coveted my mother." And then, "Damn you, Rob Zanermann for having Larry Boynton, a very sweet man, murdered out of your jealous love for me. I know I do share some of the guilt on this, but I still curse your soul."

"Marsha Zanermann."

"Dear God, please expunge all evil residing in my son, Robert, and do your will to punish Edward Zanermann, who summoned the beast to Willard Notch." And then," Beverly Poschner, I am so sorry that you and Carl got destroyed by my husband's lust."

"Wendy Zanermann."

"Dad, I now applaud my mother for leaving you!" And then, "Rob, you destroyed someone out of blind jealous rage, and God forgive me for my role in it all."

"Ashley Seznicky."

"Die, you bastard cat." And then, "Rob Zanermann, you should not be forgiven for ending the life of Larry, a fine man with darker skin than you, but a far lighter and more beautiful soul." And then, "God bless the souls of Sue Hardesty and Mary Hardesty McGinnis and a cursed death to Mary's murderer."

"Al Fenton."

"We avenge the murders of our good citizens, and I mourn the loss of our courageous and decent Sheriff I loved like a son."

"April Dobson."

"Die cursed Jaguar, spawned by evil men, killers of the love of my life." And then, "Charles Thromeyer and Sam Kendall, one of you must die to avenge my Troy."

And then Eunice stepped forward and called out her own name:

"Eunice Dobson.

"I condemn Sam Kendall, who I know in my soul is my son's murderer, to a life of loss and pain." And then, "Oh great Warrior Gods, strike the heart of the Jaguar, and condemn it to Hell." And finally, "Cast out the malice in men's hearts towards women, and allow us all to live in harmony."

Eunice then instructed everyone to take a wooden match from April and stay in the circle, bowl in one hand, match in the other. She then lit her own match, passed around the circle igniting everyone else's with hers, and then yelling to the heavens:

"*As We Torch And Burn These Material Versions Of Our Prayers And Messages From Our Inner Beings, May Their Flames Send Out A smoke That Spreads Our Words To All Corners Of Mother Earth's Great Universe. Amen. And Beyond.*"

Puffs of smoke arising from the eight burning bowls were sped upward by the wind into the darkness of the Fall New Hampshire night. For several moments, all members of the group were gazing skyward, and a few murmuring some final personal words of prayer. Then each came to Eunice, giving her a hug and their very sincere "thank you"s, and then heading for their vehicles, as April and Eunice were putting out the remaining flames of their spiritual campfire.

April asked Eunice ,"Do you want to set up another meeting before they go?"

Eunice pondered the question briefly, and then said, "No. I think our work is done. Let's just allow the forces we set in motion to do their things. I think we're all going to be okay. No, more than okay, splendid. We're all going to be splendid."

April focused her gaze on her mother-in-law, and for the first time was struck by this incredible aging woman's beauty, grace, and wisdom that were so clearly etched into every part of her. April struggled to remember exactly how Eunice had looked earlier that day, and concluded that somehow she looked different in the moonlight this night, this night that was etched into her own being. As with the others.

April grabbed Eunice and loudly declared, "I love you, Eunice Dobson."

Eunice responded with "Me, too, Darlin'. Me, too."

A long hug followed, and then each woman, united by their love for the same man, drove off into the night.

The wetness from the rain sparkled in the moonlight, and only the barking of distant dogs disturbed the silence.

Chapter 25

After

Springtime in northern New England is at best a sometimes thing, but it was early May in Willard Notch, Mother's Day to be exact, and this newly arrived Spring was already considered to be the best in years. One sunny day after another, mild temperatures, and light breezes, and the residents of Willard Notch were basking in that sun, and also in the warm glow of a town getting back to normal after surviving the darkest episode in its history just six months ago.

While no one in town could possibly have forgotten the horrors of that episode, the good feelings that come from having so successfully survived it all permeated the Notch, and everyone seemed to know in their hearts and souls that this was indeed a new day. No one seemed to question that the feelings of safety that pervaded the town were based on genuine changes in their lives, and not just wishful thinking or denial. While the total absence of crime (except for some parking tickets, several cases of driving with an expired license, and an incident involving a property dispute and "failure to show" in the ensuing court case) was an important part of this recovery, the larger part was due to what felt like a significant shift in the demeanor of Willard Notch's men in their interactions with women. Some women joked that someone must have slipped Prozac into the town's drinking water, or at least into the beer. Believers in Eunice's plan didn't joke about it all.

* * *

Claire Dobson was sitting at her kitchen table, on her phone chatting for the first time in a while with her mother-in-law.

"I'm telling you, Eunice, Marty and I are doing really well, really."

She paused to take a sip of her diet Pepsi, and continued.

"Remember that guy we told you was thinking of having his whole Boy Scout group come by for a few self defense lessons? Well, he called Marty in the studio yesterday and told him it's a definite go. This makes us far and away the most successful martial arts program in New Hampshire and from what we can tell, in all of Northern New England. We know there are some bigger ones in Boston and Hartford and Providence, but beyond that, we're it! Some guy at the Boston Globe wants to do a story on us for their 'Around New England' Sunday section for three weeks from now. Marty's really psyched about that, believe me. How's Marty? As I've been telling you ever since December, he's been an absolute sweetheart. Yeah, it's like living with a new husband. He'll do anything I ask him to, he doesn't yell or swear much anymore, and for the first time I can totally relax when he's at the Studio, not wondering what woman he might be cozying up to. Ever since his big confessional at Christmas time, and his insisting we have that renewal of vows, he's been a changed man. We're really happy and it feels like we're really in love again like we were at the very beginning years ago. Yeah, Eunice, I know you do. Love ya', and happy Mother's Day. Bye."

Claire realized Marty would be home for lunch in just a few minutes, and pulled two bowls of salad out of the refrigerator, along with two bottles of salad dressing. Coming home for lunch every day was an offering from the "new" Marty that had pleasantly surprised Claire, since she had long suspected that lunch times at the Studio were Marty's prime time for messing with the female clientele. She was well aware that the word around town was that housewives loved getting "self defense" lessons from Marty Dobson because of the "extras" he sometimes threw in. She had always tried to look the other way regarding these habits, and she had also always been willing to forgive his temper outbursts.

Now, Marty was monitoring himself, and doing a damn good job of it.

When Marty came in, they sat on the back porch eating their salads and sipping vegetable juice she had made with their juicer machine that morning.

"Marty, I was talking to your mother before you got home, and I was telling her how happy we are, and how happy I am that you've become such a wonderful partner since Christmas time. She sounded real happy to hear that."

"Hey, thanks Claire. I'm glad you told her that, otherwise she wouldn't know. I think she always saw Troy as a good husband and me as a bad one. In fact, she saw him as better in almost every way, except martial arts. That's probably why I got into it as much as I did."

"Well, to be honest, Marty, you were not such a great husband for a lot of years."

"I know that, honey, you know I know that, like I told you this winter, I was going to make up for that and be a really good husband for you from here on out, and I have, haven't I?"

"You certainly have, baby, and I love it. But you know, I'm still not sure why the big turnaround."

"Well you know, honey, sometimes I 'm not able to figure out what triggered it either... It's like I know Troy's funeral did something to me, and then a few weeks after that it's like this wave of good loving feelings washed over me, or something. It was like some heavy dark stuff inside me just left me, and I could see you for who you really are, who you always have been, and I just couldn't see that as clearly before."

Claire jumped up from her chair and threw her arms around her Black Belt husband and hugged him tightly, planting a big kiss on his cheek.

"I love you so much, Marty."

"Me too, Claire. I love you more than ever."

They were soon in the bedroom making love, and Claire passionately clung to her man, her good man.

* * *

April, Al, and Eunice were polishing off some of April's famous lasagna, and deep in conversation.

"April, your lasagna is still the best there is at least east of the Mississippi," Al said after swallowing another delectable mouthful of what he often referred to as her "culinary gold." "But no, I still haven't heard a word from my forensics counterpart in Boston about the status of their file. I guess we still have them scratching their collective heads on the Notch serial killings case."

April and Eunice both smiled and exchanged a chuckle over Al's comment.

"Any word yet on Ted McGinnis?" he asked.

"Not a word," Eunice responded. "I spoke to Billy the other day, and of course you know he's been worried that Ted could pop up in San Diego, but not as much as a phone call. He said to say hello, you guys, and he said he's just going to assume that Ted is on an extended cruise on the Captain's schooner, and will probably fall off and drown someday."

Again, a shared chuckle, this time between Al and April.

"Do you think that house will ever sell?" April asked.

"Well I 'm sure it will eventually," Eunice replied, "but probably to an outsider. I don't think it has a lot of appeal with Notch residents."

Al and April nodded in agreement as both were putting their final mouthfuls of the lasagna.

"April, honey, the lasagna was perfect, and god bless this strong coffee, because Al and I are going to see that new movie about outer space, and you know how draggy those can be."

"Yeah," Al quipped, "but this one is supposed to be pretty exciting from what I've heard. But I'll bet you'll be wide awake at three in the morning with all that caffeine."

"Yeah, Al, and if I am I'll bet I won't get any complaints from you," Eunice retorted.

Al smiled, turned a little pink, and simply said, "That's true."

He still felt awkward about the budding romance he and Eunice had been sharing since the big night at the football field, now known as the home of The Willard Notch Panthers. The School Board did the renaming at the request of Billy McGinnis, who served as spokesperson for the group about the atrocious historical realities of the Jaguars in Willard Notch. When he spoke of the panther as simply a blood brother of the jaguar but with a more acceptable packaging for the Notch, everyone was supportive of the idea.

In any case, Al and Eunice always liked each other as acquaintances, but Eunice was his boss's mother, and he figured not suitable for dating. And besides, Al never had any thoughts of dating anyway.

But the shared participation by the two senior citizens in the process of saving the town, brought them a truckload of mutual respect, and a heightened sense of connectedness. In fact, it seemed like everyone at the field that night got that same feeling of almost a kinship, a feeling that would last their entire lives.

Word was that Wendy was quite happy living with her mother and Andy and had grown to really appreciate Handy Randy Andy as a very nice man.

A s for her brother, he and she exchanged birthday and Hanukkah cards, as did Marsha, but that seemed to be all he ever wanted with them... or anyone. He was still living in that same house, and kept Zanermann's Men's Store going after Ed left town for parts unknown. But everyone in town knew the business was failing badly, and that Rob would have to sell it for a loss before long, and the house, too.

Kendall Motors was now in receivership after Sam's sudden and violent death on Valentine's Day. It seems he was out at a Manchester night club with Marge Thromeyer, even though he was supposedly very depressed over Sarah's rather suspicious disappearance, and he somehow managed to choke to death on a chicken bone. The word was it was a wishbone of all things.

As for Jan and Ashley, they continue to be very close, and in fact Eunice had just gotten a postcard from Negril, Jamaica where both of them were now on vacation, saying they had decided to extend their stay by at least four more days and a week if they could work it. Jamaican sun, sand, sea, and sexy guys were keeping them very happy, and they asked her to tell Billy that absolutely no one drinks Captain Morgan's down there.

So here they were, the three *amigos*, taking their final bites of that best lasagna in the eastern half of America, feeling quite content with where that apocalyptic night had brought them, and what it had brought to Willard Notch, New Hampshire.

"April, honey, I am about to steal your terrific mother-in-law away from you right now, or we'll be late for our movie at the Strand. Thanks for the feast, and I'll see you tomorrow."

"Enjoy," April smilingly responded. "You, too, Mom."

She watched as these two caring elder souls went out the door, smiling with her own loving approval. Where that relationship might head didn't really matter. They were well connected and good to each other, and that was what really mattered.

Her thoughts drifted to Troy as she threw the three empty pie plates and paper cups into the large trash can near her desk. Troy was a good man... Perfect? No, and she had months ago decided she'll never know what happened with Troy and Marge that fateful day at Kendall's, certain that she will never ask. She was a great believer that if there was a high probability you could end up sorry you asked about something, don't ask.

All she knew is that Troy was always very good to her in so many ways, and that she would love him until the day she dies, and if she can, she wants to be buried with an unopened bottle of Arrow Coffee Brandy, in case she meets up with him.

Brushing away a few tears, she glanced down at the shiny star pinned to her tan shirt and at the "Sheriff Dobson" nameplate on her desk, and April Dobson, Menard County's first woman Sheriff, headed for one of her file cabinets.

It was just another work day in Willard Notch, New Hampshire.

Part V

EPILOGUE

Chapter 26

And Beyond

Antoinette Faison was dead, stone cold dead by the time Detective Archie Frechette arrived on the scene. The first Baton Rouge cop to arrive had responded to an emergency call from her son, Bucky, who said in the call that he had found her dead on the living room floor when he got home after closing his liquor store, He said she wasn't bleeding or anything, but she was purplish, and he figured she was already gone. He said the only unusual thing was that her left leg was swollen to twice the size of her right leg. When the officer saw the body, he immediately called Detective Frechette, The BRPD's reigning expert on this type of case.

"Hey Archie? Bobby Lee Carton here. Hey, look, I got a weird case here where I need your help. Yeah. It's old Mrs. Faison, Bucky's mom. She's lying here dead on her living room floor, and damned if one of her legs isn't swole up to twice it's normal size. Sure looks like a snake bite to me. We searched the house just now and didn't see no sign of a snake anywhere. And then I started to think, Jeez, when was the last time we found a case of a death from a poisonous snake bite in their own home, and how come she never called us or Bucky for help while there was still time, you know?"

Detective Frechette said he'd be right over, and he was. He ended up as puzzled as Bobby Lee, and remained so even after interviewing Bucky. He made sure a blood sample was taken for the forensics lab, and that appropriate crime scene procedures were followed, even though he had to agree with Bucky that it really wasn't clear that there had been a crime. As he headed home for the night, Frechette felt that something wasn't right about the case, and next day feedback from the forensics lab confirmed this.

The next morning he learned from the folks at Forensics that with all the cottonmouths, rattlers, water moccasins, and god only knows what else in nearby swamp country, the blood sample actually matched up with viper toxin, a very unusual finding.

Archie was now sure this was going to be one hell of a weird case.

In another part of the city, where it had just begun to rain in that torrential tropical storm downpour style that plagued Louisiana, Christine Madore was being questioned by an Emergency Unit doctor and nurse at Baton Rouge City Hospital.

"Mrs. Madore. Christine. Are you telling us once again that you tripped over one of your kids toys and hit your head on their toy box? How many times have you already told us that this year? I'm sure if your house had a basement you'd be telling us you tripped going down the cellar stairs. You do know that the gash on the side of your head is a bad one, and that you have a concussion, right?"

"Dr. Ewing, I'm telling you the truth, and now I have to get back home for my kids."

"Okay, Christine, okay. Listen, is Arnold home? You know the procedure, and the cops are going to want to talk with him."

"Yeah, I know the procedure, but he's not at home, and I haven't seen him since yesterday. Sorry, I gotta go."

Yeah, Christine, I understand," and Will Ewing's face showed profound sadness as he headed back to the ER nursing station.

And in her living room, Donna Desjardins was tearfully explaining to two Baton Rouge policemen how worried she was about her teen age daughter, Bessie, who hadn't slept in her bed and hadn't been seen all day and evening. This was very unusual behavior for her because she had slept at home every night of her fourteen year life, and always left a note for Donna whenever she went anywhere. The officers tried reassuring her that Bessie was likely just off with her friends somewhere, but that in any case, they would have to wait until morning to begin a missing person investigation.

They asked her if she needed anything before they left, given the fact that she was blind, and home alone since Guy had died from prostate cancer six months ago. She assured them all she needed was to have her Bessie home safe.

It was raining even harder as the two got into their cruiser.

"What a terrible night!" one said to the other.

"Sure is!" he concurred, neither one knowing just how right they were.

* * *

Not the End

About the Author

Ralph Zieff is a retired mental health professional with 48 years of practice behind him, and now living in a Maine retirement community. He began writing in his mid-seventies with "Reaching For The Stars",an autobiographical account of his many years as an autograph seeker.His second book is "Chasing Darkness", a thriller novel about "love and evil".He is currently writing a book about racism in America, and plans to follow it with a novel about severe spousal abuse. He is the father of three (all with health care professions) and seven grandchildren ranging in age from eight to eighteen, He attended Harvard in the Timothy Leary and Baba Ram Das years, which helped shape him into the free-thinking and slightly idiosyncratic person he is today. His great loves these days, besides writing and eating, are the Boston Red Sox, hard bop jazz, reggae, and Broadway musicals.

Books by the Author

Chasing Darkness
Reaching For The Stars: Impressions, Obsessions and Confessions of an Old Autograph Hound
Willard Notch

Lightning Source UK Ltd.
Milton Keynes UK
UKHW021823191120
373696UK00003B/490